KILTS
AND
Kisses

VICTORIA ROBERTS

PUBLISHED BY:
Victoria Roberts

KILTS AND KISSES

Copyright © 2015 by Victoria Roberts

Cover Design and Interior format by The Killion Group
http://thekilliongroupinc.com

DEDICATION

To wee Jamie, the newest addition to our clan. Ye'll always be our little pirate. *Aargh!*

CHAPTER ONE

Scottish Highlands, 1607

"She's a witch."

"Anna, contrary to whatever ye are thinking in that wee brain of yours, our aunt is nay witch. She believes heavily in superstition. There's a difference."

Ceana Gunn stood on the parapet of her home as a cool breeze combed through her loose tendrils. She closed her eyes and prayed for patience. There were days when her fifteen-year-old sister drove her completely mad. And this was one of those times. Ceana gazed out at her father's lands, deep in thought.

The mossy fields were a lovely shade of green, and dappled purple heather reached up from the grass as if asking the sun to carry it away in a warm embrace. A hawk glided fluidly through the air and then swooped down to capture its latest prey. In the distance, the forest line encircling the loch was lush with pine trees and foliage.

How Ceana wished she could escape there now.

She missed the much simpler pleasures of her youth and longed for peace and solitude, away from everything and everyone. When her brief moment of solace was interrupted again by her sister's endless prattle, Ceana mentally suppressed a sigh.

"But Aunt Marta said birds bring about death. How would she know that if she wasnae a witch?"

Ceana didn't want to tell Anna that if she didn't stop talking, she'd bring about her own demise, but the last thing Ceana wanted was for her sister to be as superstitious as their aunt. "Ye cannae take everything Aunt Marta says as the truth. Besides, she doesnae feel that way about all birds—only crows, ye know."

Anna put her hands on the stone wall. Leaning forward over the edge, her long, blond locks caught in the gentle wind. "Do ye think 'tis safe to go down now?"

"I think we should wait until we're certain the company have taken their leave. Mayhap then our dear cousin Sorcha will nae be vying for so much attention and making such a fool of herself. 'Tis hard to believe she is a Gunn and shares our blood."

"Aye, we should wait." Anna brushed down the blue day dress that complemented her ivory skin. The color of the fabric matched her azure eyes, and the hues of the sky made her look as though she was painted onto an artist's canvas. She was the picture of their mother.

"I donna understand why Sorcha acts the way she

does." Anna continued with her commentary to Ceana's dismay. "I think she forgets that we all used to play together as children. I donna know what has happened to her. She isnae the same person. She's changed, and nae for the better I tell ye." Anna took a short breath.

"Why do ye think Aunt Marta and Uncle John treat her differently than us? They let her have anything she wants. All Sorcha has to do is ask. And ye've seen her trunks. How many gowns can one woman have before 'tis enough? When was the last time Aunt Marta had dresses made for us, eh?"

Ceana gave her sister a wry grin. "Of course Aunt Marta and Uncle John treat Sorcha differently. She's their daughter."

Anna let out a primal growl. "Mayhap, but times like these make me realize how much I miss our mother and father. What I wouldnae give to have them here with us now."

"I know, Sister. I miss them too."

Ceana straightened her spine and willed the tears not to fall. Although two years should've been ample time to erase memories of the past, the circumstances of her parents' deaths still haunted her. Most of the time she had a hard time acknowledging that her mother and father were no longer of this world.

A thoughtful smile curved Ceana's mouth as she remembered the gleam in her mother's eyes every time the woman laid eyes on her husband. And how could she forget the loving gesture of her father's hand placed at her mother's back every time her parents walked side by side? The two of them had been inseparable, but knowing she'd never be able to see them again was like having her beating heart impaled by a sharp dagger.

"I see the look on your face, Ceana. Donna try to hide it. Ye recognize the truth for what it is. If Father and Mother werenae killed by those vagrants who robbed them on the road, Father would still be laird. And ye know verra well that *ye* would now be the one foolishly vying for attention, not Sorcha." When Ceana pursed her lips, Anna added, "I know. Ye would ne'er behave the way that Sorcha does. But does it nae trouble ye?"

Ceana became uneasy under her sister's scrutiny and shifted her weight. "There is naught we can do to change the past. We need to look toward the future and nae look behind. That's what Mother and Father would've wanted for us." Turning her head away from her prying sister, Ceana stared blankly into the courtyard below, refusing to admit that Anna was right.

A loud commotion came from the bailey, causing Anna to glance over the wall. "I think 'tis safe to return. The latest suitor has taken his leave."

"Let us give thanks to God for small favors. I donna know how many more of these visits I can bear."

When Ceana and Anna entered the great hall, servants were working to clear the long wooden table on the dais of meats, breads, and cheeses—but not before Anna managed to grab a handful of food. She didn't even wait to sit down before she broke off a piece of bread and gobbled it down.

"I'm famished," she said. "At least there's something remaining for us to eat this time. Ye better grab a bite before 'tis too late. How many more suitors do ye think will come before these men clean us out of our stores for the winter?"

"I see the two of ye managed to find your way back. More's the pity, if ye ask me."

Anna's eyes blazed with anger. "We *didnae* ask ye."

"Sorcha, ye look lovely." Ceana made every effort to mask the look of contempt that crossed her face. Too bad her cousin's comeliness didn't outweigh her dreadful demeanor. Ceana had to fight an internal battle every day to make certain that Sorcha's abhorrent behavior wasn't contagious.

Her cousin's newest gown was gold and trimmed with blackwork embroidery. The neck opening was filled in with a linen partlet, and a ribbon sash was secured at Sorcha's slender waist. Her ash-brown hair clustered in short curls around her oval face, the same face that currently studied Ceana from head to toe.

"Mother had this gown made for me. I think 'tis rather fitting for the occasion. Wouldnae ye say?"

Anna huffed. *"I'd* say ye—"

"Aye. 'Tis quite lovely."

Sorcha glared at Anna. "Ye two will nae ruin this

for me. Do ye hear me?"

"Ruin this for ye?" Anna's voice went up a notch. "If nae for my father, there would be naught—"

"*Na can an còrr! Tha sin gu leòr!*" *Say no more! That is enough!* "Good heavens, child. I can hear all of ye from across the hall. There is nay need for these constant squabbles." Aunt Marta placed silvery locks of hair behind her ear and then smoothed her red skirts. She was a petite woman with a square chin and a wide mouth that looked large for such a small frame.

"Our guest has departed. Take your leave and wash your sleeve," she said, wrapping her fingers around the gold fabric of Sorcha's dress.

"I donna see any dirt on Sorcha's dress."

Aunt Marta raised her hands to Anna's cheeks. "Och, lassie. I know her dress isnae soiled. Sorcha is going to find out which suitor will take her to wife."

"My apologies, but I donna understand."

"'Tisnae your fault that your mother didnae teach ye such things." Aunt Marta lowered her arms and gave Anna a patient smile. "'Tis said that if a maiden travels to a south-running stream, to a ford where the dead and the living cross, she's to wash her sleeve in the water. When she returns home, she's to hang the garment in front of the fire and keep a careful eye. If Sorcha watches closely, she'll see the apparition of her future husband when he comes to turn the wet cloth."

Anna's jaw dropped. "Ye're jesting with me."

"Oh, on the contrary, I'm quite serious, my dear. That's exactly how I knew I was destined to wed your Uncle John. Now that's enough of this quarreling, all of ye. I've heard enough to last the rest of my days." Aunt Marta turned on her heel as Sorcha rested her gaze on Ceana.

"Let me make something clear to the both of ye," their cousin said. "I will wed the most powerful laird in the Highlands to benefit our clan because I am the laird's daughter. My marriage will bring with it alliances and prosperity for many generations to come. So the two of ye better nae do anything foolish. And if ye continue to put obstacles in my path, I'll nae only remove them, I'll remove the both of ye."

As Sorcha waved her hand in a dismissive gesture and bristled off, Anna poked her elbow into Ceana's arm. "What are we going to do about her?"

"I donna know, but if she doesnae mind her words, I'm going to throttle her."

"I'm glad to hear it because frankly, I've been fretting over ye lately, Sister. Ye've put up with Sorcha's vile behavior long enough. I'm relieved to see ye still have some of Father's tenacity within ye."

Ceana lifted a brow. "Father? I assure ye that I am my mother's daughter. Ye donna remember all the times Mother put Uncle John in his place when he disagreed with the decisions Father had made for the clan?"

"Uncle John? Nay. When?"

"'Tisnae important. What is important is that ye

continue with your studies. There is nay greater gift than the gift of knowledge."

Ceana lit the candles in her bedchamber, donned her nightrail, and drew back the heavy curtains to see moonlight shining through the slit in the stone wall. Leaning closer, she looked through the hole. The moon was full and high in the night sky.

She sat on the bed and pulled out her journal from under the feather mattress. As she opened the page to the entry she'd made from the evening before, she sighed. Sorcha was two years younger than Ceana and only a year older than Anna. So why were Uncle John and Aunt Marta arranging a marriage for Sorcha now? Her cousin had said the words herself. She was the laird's daughter. It didn't matter how old Ceana was because her father was dead. She was no longer the laird's daughter. That right now belonged to Sorcha, a fact she wouldn't let Ceana forget any time soon.

Glancing down at her journal, Ceana didn't see any words on the page. That revelation came as no surprise. She knew she'd never be able to pen a single word this eve. She closed the book and placed it on the bed. Bringing her knees to her chest, she rested her chin on top and closed her eyes.

"*Fuirich mionaid.*" *Wait a moment.* "I refuse to let Sorcha plague me. 'Tis madness." Ceana flew to her feet, donned her slippers, grabbed her cloak from the corner chair, and bolted out the door. She needed air and would not permit herself to be suffocated by her own dire thoughts.

Making her way through the halls of the castle, she saw that the main torches were extinguished, but a few remained lit to guide her. She knew the servants had retired to their chambers long ago. As she was passing the wall where her father's portrait used to hang, she scoffed at her Uncle John's likeness that now hung in its place. Becoming even more incensed, she walked with long, purposeful strides. She couldn't reach her destination soon enough.

She climbed the narrow, winding steps to the parapet. It was engulfed in blackness, which suited her darkened mood fine. The only reason she didn't fall and break her neck was because she placed her hands on the stone walls at each side to guide her. When she reached the top of the stairs, she opened the door.

Ceana stood in the same spot she always did, and the moon was so bright that it illuminated her father's lands. She could even see the shadows of the tree line in the distance. The moon cast an eerie glow across the moors, as if the veil was thin between this world and the next. That was the moment she realized that she'd heard enough of Aunt Marta's constant ramblings about specters and the fae. She whipped her head to the right as the sound of a sword scraped against the wall.

"I love to kiss ye. Ye taste as sweet as honey."

"And I bet ye say that to all the lasses."

"There are nay other lasses, Anna, only ye."

Ceana's body stiffened in shock. She hesitated longer than she should have, but then darted back to the stairs. Standing as still as a statue in the darkness, she leaned against the parapet door. God's teeth! What was Anna doing up here at this time of night?

Ceana knew the answer to the question, but that didn't prevent it from coming to mind. With all her might, she resisted the urge to walk over there and demand to know everything. What man would be so cocksure as to hold Anna in his arms under their sire's roof? Surely he couldn't be one of her father's guards because those men knew better.

As the voices came closer, Ceana made her way carefully down the stairs. She tried to move as fast as she could in the blackness, but when she heard a step behind her, she froze. Not only that, but her foot almost missed the step entirely. She took a moment to still her wild, beating heart.

"Will I see ye on the morrow?" asked Anna.

"Shhh…*dèan air do shocair.*" *Be quiet.*

"All right, but answer my question."

"Aye. I have to ride out to the border, but *cha bhi mi fada.*" *I won't be long.* "Meet me here. I'll be waiting for ye, as always."

There was a brief pause.

"*Mar sin leat.*" *Good-bye.*

"*Chi mi a-màireach.*" *I'll see you tomorrow.* "Until we meet again…"

Ceana walked with hurried purpose through the halls to Anna's bedchamber. Once inside, she paced. What was her sister thinking? How long had Anna been meeting this man? More to the point, how could Ceana not have known? The door opened, and Anna's voice rose in surprise.

"What are ye doing in my chamber at this time of night?"

"And I could verra well ask ye why ye arenae *in* your chamber at this time of night. Who was that man?"

"What man?"

Ceana wasn't fooled by the innocent expression that crossed her sister's face. "Ye know darn well what man. The man on the parapet who couldnae separate his lips from yours."

"Oh, that man." Anna stepped around Ceana with an air of indifference. "'Tis Calum's son."

"Raonull, the rogue?"

"Raonull? I am nay fool. 'Tis Samuel."

Even though Ceana felt relief knowing the man on the parapet was not the biggest rogue in the castle, her stomach still soured at the thought of Anna in the arms of Raonull's brother. After all, who knew what the rogue had taught his younger brother about women. "Please tell me ye still have your virtue."

Anna sat on the bed and folded her arms across her chest. "I cannae believe ye would ask that of me." When Ceana waited for an answer, Anna added, "Of course I do. I am nae daft, and by all means, I am nay harlot."

"How long?"

"How long *what?*"

Ceana sat beside Anna on the bed and took a deep breath. "How long have ye been meeting Samuel?"

"Only for a fortnight. He's verra kind to me, Ceana. He doesnae want to cause trouble. He cares for me, and he's a good man."

"I donna like it."

Anna smiled, patting Ceana on the thigh. "Be truthful. Would ye like anyone who courted me?"

"Nay, but that doesnae matter. If Aunt Marta or Uncle John, or even Sorcha, finds out ye've been meeting with Samuel in the darkened hours of the night—"

"They will nae. We're verra careful." Anna took Ceana's hand. "Please. Ever since Mother and Father passed, there has been nay light in our lives. This is the first time that I find a smile on my face. Ye know it doesnae hurt to smile once in a while, eh? Mayhap if ye found a man too—"

Ceana waved her sister off. "If I sought companionship, I'd seek out one of the castle dogs."

"Mother and Father are gone. They're nae coming back."

There was a heavy silence.

"Since when does my younger sister find the need to counsel me? Ye donna need to tell me they're nae coming back. I know."

"Be that as it may, I know our parents would've

expected ye to live your life. Ye need to smile, laugh... I cannae remember the last time I saw any of that from ye. There is naught we can do about Sorcha and her annoying suitors, but once she weds 'the most powerful laird in the Highlands,' she will nay longer be underfoot and causing trouble. For the moment, cannae ye be happy for me? I need this—Samuel—in my life."

"Let me get some sleep and we'll talk about it on the morrow. But give me your word there will be nay more secret meetings with Samuel."

"*A-mach à seo!" Out of here!* "I cannae give my word for something I cannae do."

Ceana stood. "I'm going to bed. I've had more than enough this eve."

"Do ye think she waits?"

"Pardon?"

"Sorcha. Do ye think she waits for the apparition of her future husband to appear in her bedchamber?"

"I think any man—or apparition—who is willing to take Sorcha to wife is a daft fool."

"Ye still donna believe Aunt Marta is a witch, do ye?"

Ceana wiped her hand across her brow. "I think Aunt Marta believes in some verra strange things, but nay, she is nay witch. Ye best keep those thoughts to yourself. Get some sleep, Anna." Ceana closed the door behind her and briefly closed her eyes. Not only were suitors scaling the walls in order to gain her sixteen-year-old cousin's favor, but now Ceana had discovered that her fifteen-year-old sister was having nightly trysts on the parapet.

Perhaps it was time that this eighteen-year-old lass did something different for a change.

CHAPTER TWO

Luthais MacKay reveled in the silence that surrounded him. He tilted his neck from left to right. As the cool night air blew tendrils of hair into his face, he secured the loose strands behind his ear. He took another swig of whisky and then wiped his mouth with the back of his hand. Since he was a small boy, he had often found solace in this spot.

The full moon cast a shimmering glow on the water as if it taunted him, making him believe this was the last moment of peace he'd ever receive. He rubbed his fingers over his tired eyes. In his sire's absence, the clan felt compelled to have Luthais settle disputes. And not just any disputes—the petty kind over sheep and rents, and how could he forget the incident of the clansman who was cuckolded by his wife?

The men demanded justice. They couldn't even wait until his father returned from Edinburgh before they swarmed like a bunch of bees, sensing sweet nectar and then turning around and stinging Luthais in the arse. Then again, perhaps he shouldn't be too eager to see Laird William MacKay. After all, his father would not be pleased when he found the clan in such disarray, although Luthais had tried his best to act in his father's stead.

He gazed up when he felt eyes watching him from the tree branch overhead. "I know ye're there."

The only response was the sound of fluttering wings.

"How could ye know? I made nay sound."

A figure approached in the moonlight, and Luthais held back a groan. If he didn't know better, he would've been taken aback by the red-haired man who stood six and a half feet tall and carried a broadsword. "What are ye doing? I came out here to be alone."

"What kind of man would I be to let my best lad drink alone? I've come to share your drink." Doughall extended his hand for the flask and then took a swig.

Luthais knew when a battle was already lost. There was no sense in arguing for his friend to depart. Lowering himself to the ground, Luthais rested his back against the standing stones that had been there for centuries. He'd never understood the significance of the rocks, if any, but they were a common staple of the Scottish landscape. Although some clan members believed the formations had been left by the fae, others thought they were a relic left for young lovers to seal their devotion to each other. He wasn't foolish enough to believe in such superstitions. But for some unexplainable reason, six giant rocks formed a circle on MacKay lands at the northern end of the loch.

"I'm afraid to ask, but how did ye find me?"

Doughall sat beside Luthais and handed back the whisky. "Ye're always at *na tursachan* when ye're troubled." *The standing stones.* "What will ye do when your father returns on the morrow?"

"Gladly hand back the reins."

"Ye know what I mean."

"Aye. I donna know. He will be cross."

Doughall laughed. "Think ye?"

"I donna want to talk about it. I came out here to drink in peace. *Na can an còrr.*" *Say no more.*

"I will nae stop ye from getting into your cups, but I suggest your head be clear for thought when ye speak to your father."

Luthais let the fiery liquid burn down his throat. "Aye, well, I'll worry about that on the morrow."

"God's teeth!" Doughall eyed the trees above with disgust and then wiped his shoulder. "Why do your vexatious birds always shite on me?"

"They know the hand that feeds them."

"Be that as it may, mayhap ye can train them a wee bit better, eh? They're only as good as the man who trains them."

"I'll think about it. Do ye have anything to eat? I didnae sup."

"Aye…mutton."

"Arse. I told ye that I donna want to hear another word about the damn sheep."

A flash of humor crossed Doughall's face. "Baaah."

"Ye know ye would've done the same."

Doughall shrugged. "In truth, ye did more than I would have done." He gave Luthais a brotherly punch in the arm. "If it were me, I would've told the men to keep their squabbling to themselves and wait for the damn laird to return. But then again, I am nae the laird's son and the one who had to listen to the whining in my ear every day."

"I donna know how my father does it. Who would've thought the MacKays could be so annoying?" When Doughall lifted his brow and gave him a knowing look, Luthais stood with the whisky in hand. "Bastard. I'm going home where I can find air to breathe. Do ye stay?"

"Och, nay. I'll return with ye." Doughall pulled himself to his feet at the same time Luthais extended his arms in the air as if to embrace the moon.

"*Trobhadaidh.*" *Come.* As the branches rustled overhead, he couldn't help but chuckle when the mighty Doughall took a step back. Luthais ambled toward his mount as several talons descended upon him, gripping the leather straps on his shoulders and the one on his forearm.

Laird William MacKay sat behind the desk in his study. He always had an authoritative manner, which was why he was a powerful laird. But this time his coolness was evidence that he was not amused. With his square jaw tensed, he exuded an air of command. Although Luthais' sire used to have a wealth of red hair, those strands had grayed at the temples and looked unruly. Still dressed in his traveling clothes, his father didn't even bother to remove the dust from his plaid before he called Luthais in to face the inquisition.

"Ye did what?"

Luthais winced. "Father, please let me explain."

"Ye better have a damn good reason... God's teeth! What explanation could ye possibly give? Are ye daft? Sometimes I wonder if ye're truly my son. I have nay doubt that your lack of judgment comes from your mother's kin." He paused. "Och, well, at least the lass had enough sense to wed the likes of me."

Luthais shifted in the chair and gazed at the shield and swords that hung behind his father's head. Perhaps it wasn't too late to grab something off the wall in order to defend himself from his father's wrath. But when he saw the fire return in his sire's eyes, he realized it was too late. He felt like he was a wee lad getting scolded in his father's study for the first time.

"The men wouldnae wait for your return. They came to me because they knew I acted in your stead."

"Ye should be able to act in my stead by now!" His father sighed with exasperation. "I want to know what in the hell possessed ye to do this." Luthais was about to speak when his father held up his hand to stay him. "But more to the point, why did ye tie a rope around Dhoileag and John, and then tie one of John's sheep to Thomas and have all of them walk around the village like a damn procession? *Có thusa*?" *Who are you?*

When his father phrased it that way, Luthais realized perhaps that hadn't been one of his best ideas. A lump formed in his throat. "Ye see, Father, John and Thomas plagued me every day of your absence. Thomas claimed Dhoileag had cuckolded him with John, and John said Thomas stole his sheep. I held off as long as I could for your return and grew tired of hearing their endless words about one another. I wasnae sure who to believe. There was nay proof that Dhoileag shared her favors with another man, and I wasnae certain Thomas stole John's sheep. I donna think ye would've wanted me to cut off Thomas's hand and John's bollocks without knowing the truth."

His father rubbed his brow. "So ye bound them all together like haggis in the middle of the village and they walked around like idiots?"

"Aye, but they only had to stay that way until one of them spoke the truth, or they saw to it to forget this matter."

"But if 'tis true and Dhoileag wasnae faithful to her husband, Thomas's honor is at stake. Justice must be served."

"And what would ye have me do, Father? *Is*

iomadh rud a nì dithis dheònach." Two willing people can do many things.

His father's expression became pained. "How do ye expect to take my place one day as laird when ye make such foolish decisions? The men looked to ye to pass judgment. They expected ye to consider their words and didnae expect ye to make a mockery of their grievances. Ye are my only heir. If I die on the morrow, I cannae say that I would blame the clan for choosing Doughall over ye to be chief."

"Doughall? He doesnae want to be laird. His only purpose is proving to everyone that he's the best warrior in all the Highlands."

"This conversation is long past due." There was an edge to his father's voice. "Ye know King James demands that the lairds travel to Edinburgh every year. Ye need to show the clan that ye're able to make wise decisions in my absence. And contrary to what ye might think, tying a sheep to a thief and a wife to her lover isnae one of them. Ye need to think in the best interest of the clan, always. That's what makes a good chief. 'Tis time to change, Luthais." His father stood.

"Ye need to think of someone other than yourself." He paused, tapping his finger on the desk and staring at it in a trance-like state. "Your mother was a good woman. Mayhap that is what ye need."

"I donna understand."

"A woman, one woman. Mayhap what ye need is a wife. Ye're one and twenty. What better way to learn to be accountable for someone else than to have a wife?"

"Surely ye're jesting." Luthais knew his father was not.

"I've heard rumors that Laird Gunn seeks a husband for his daughter. Your marriage could bring an alliance between our clans."

"I'm able to have a wife of my own choosing."

"Then do so before I choose for ye."

Luthais stiffened as though his father had struck him. He knew his sire was tired of his careless behavior, but another pecking bird in his life was not what he wanted or needed. At least his own birds minded him. "Father—"

"I just returned from Edinburgh and once again had to clean up your mess. I want to bathe. I want to eat. And I am done talking." The laird walked around the desk and held up his hand, giving fair warning when he passed and walked out the door.

"Damn."

"What did he say?"

Luthais looked over his shoulder and growled at his friend who had just entered the room. "He wants me to wed."

There was a heavy silence.

"I see that look in your eyes, Doughall. Out with it."

"As I said before, I'm thankful I'm nae the laird's son," his friend said with a chuckle.

"That's all ye have to say? Ye have nay advice to

offer me?"

Doughall shrugged. "I wish ye luck with that."

Luthais rode through the village, continued through the glen, and then made his way to the loch. He tied off his faithful mount, a beast of an animal. The sturdy chestnut warhorse never hesitated when given a command. Gazing around the loch, Luthais watched as one of his hawks skimmed the surface of the water with its talons and flew into a nearby tree. Luthais climbed the small, grassy knoll, realizing he hadn't been here in the daylight for a long time. He always favored brooding alone in the darkness. But as he reached the standing stones, he stopped dead in his tracks.

A woman sat with her back resting against his favorite rock. Her light-brown hair hung in loose waves over her shoulder and her brow was furrowed. She was so engrossed in the small journal she was reading that she didn't hear him approach.

"Ye're clearly nae reading about the MacKays or ye'd know ye were trespassing on our lands."

Emerald eyes met his, and without warning, he felt like he'd been punched in the gut by Doughall. The woman closed the book and rose, smoothing the skirts of her day dress. The apricot and milky shades of her skin reminded him of light-colored cream. She had a genial mouth and sparkling eyes. When the wind picked up, tousling her brown locks, the faint smile that she gave him held a touch of sadness. Her steps slowed as she walked toward him. From her demeanor, she looked as though she could be as playful as a young lass or as composed as an intelligent woman.

"Please accept my apologies. I was just about to take my leave." She walked past him and around the circle of standing stones.

"And where do ye think ye're going?"

She laughed over her shoulder. "Mayhap ye're the one who needs to pick up a book. I told ye I was about to take my leave."

"*Dé'n t-ainm a th'ort?*" *What's your name?* When she paid him no heed and continued to place distance between them, he added, "*Fuirich mionaid!*" *Wait a moment!* Luthais ran to catch up with her. He grabbed her arm and turned her to face him. When she gripped the journal to her chest in a protective embrace, he instinctively rested his hand on the hilt of his sword.

Her eyes widened. "Surely ye donna think I'm going to cause ye harm. Now if ye'll excuse me, I'll be taking my leave."

His hand came down on her shoulder as she tried to turn away from him again. "Are ye alone?"

"And what gave me away, pray tell?" She exhaled with agitation.

"Ye have a sharp tongue."

Her slender hand touched his forearm. "Please accept my apologies. I only sought peace and quiet. I'm afraid I've made a mistake. I will nae come here again. Ye have my word."

She grabbed the reins of her horse and mounted with ease as Luthais stood there like a dolt, trying to figure out why he didn't move to stop her. In fact, he found himself at an actual loss for words, which was a rare occurrence.

"Ye didnae tell me your name."

She straightened her shoulders and lowered her eyes to his. "Nay, I didnae."

The lass kicked her mount into a gallop. Thundering hoofbeats pounded the earth around the loch and into the dense forest. Luthais didn't tear his eyes away until the woman passed out of sight. He'd never seen her before. Where did she come from? He couldn't answer that question, but he knew the answer to another.

She'd set foot on his enemy's lands.

CHAPTER THREE

The wind whipped through her hair. A branch slapped her in the face. A thorn scratched her leg, and yet Ceana didn't slow her horse. She needed to place as much distance between herself and that man as she could. Uncle John would serve her head on a platter if she was caught trespassing on MacKay lands. She turned her head over her shoulder, praying she wasn't being followed.

Who knew what had drawn her to the standing stones in the first place, but she wouldn't make that mistake again. She'd always remained on Gunn property around the loch. But her father's lands were becoming far too crowded with Sorcha's admirers of late. She needed a change of venue to escape the chaos inside and out. When her mind wandered back to the guard who caught her where she wasn't supposed to be, she shuddered. Thank God she was able to talk him into letting her leave of her own free will.

The MacKay guard was an imposing man,

especially with the large broadsword that was sheathed at his waist. She could barely remember his features because her only thought at the time was escape. But she did notice that he wore a blue, green, and black kilt and had leather straps on his shoulders and forearms. He was battle ready. She tried to keep that in the back of her mind because the next time she saw the tartan, she'd be sure to flee. Not that there would be a next time, but perhaps his companions wouldn't be as kind.

Ceana slowed her pace when she cleared the trees. For once, her home was a welcome sight. She suddenly longed for the security of the stone walls, even with mad Aunt Marta and haughty Sorcha. In a way, her experience with the MacKay guard had both thrilled her and frightened her. She wasn't sure how that was possible.

As soon as she entered the bailey, Anna walked hurriedly toward her.

"Ceana, make haste."

"What has happened?" She dismounted, handing the reins to the stable hand. She knew her short-lived adventure was over because she was instantly thrown back into her disorderly life.

"Come with me, and we'll kill her together."

Ceana followed Anna through the great hall. Seeing the servants readying the midday meal, Ceana prayed that the food on the tables wasn't for another one of her cousin's suitors. As the sisters climbed the stairs to their private rooms, Anna spoke over her shoulder.

"'Tis Sorcha. She ransacked your bedchamber searching for one of her dresses. She's mad. She thinks ye took her gown because ye admired it."

When they reached Ceana's room, they found Aunt Marta standing in the hall in front of the door. Their aunt began to shake when she saw Ceana. "But if ye donna do what is right, sin is crouching at your door. It desires to have ye, but ye must master it."

Ceana placed her hand on her aunt's shoulder. "I'm afraid the only sin crouching at my door, Aunt Marta, is your daughter. I havenae taken anything of Sorcha's." Ceana entered her chamber and bit down hard on her lower lip to control her anger.

"Where is it? What have ye done?" Sorcha whipped the dress that she held to the floor and stormed toward Ceana, closing the distance between them. "Where is my gown?"

"What gown?"

"The one that I wore last eve. The one ye admired."

Anna flanked Ceana, her face a glowering mask of rage. "Leave her alone, Sorcha! She doesnae have it! *Tha sin gu leòr!*" *That is enough!*

"I donna have your dress, nor would I want it." Ceana stepped around her pampered cousin and gazed at her once well-kept room. All the clothes from her trunk were scattered about. The blankets from the bed, including her mother's golden embroidered coverlet, lay in a heap on the floor, and the edge of

Ceana's journal stuck out from under the feather mattress. But when she spotted her mother's pendant, which had been thrown across the room with complete callousness, Ceana's temper flared.

Each stride was fluid until she dropped to her knees in the corner of her chamber. She cupped the jewelry in her hand, fingering the delicate object with fond memories. This was the only piece of jewelry remaining from her mother's things. The gold pendant was set with a yellow-brown garnet and a deep yellow-green gem. A single sapphire teardrop hung on the bottom, a gift her father had given her mother on their wedding day. And her cousin had tossed the jewelry on the floor like it was nothing more than yesterday's trash.

Ceana's expression darkened, and she rose. She glared at Sorcha with burning, reproachful eyes as Aunt Marta stepped into the room, waving her arms.

"Sorcha, cease! Cannae ye see she holds the amulet? The power is within her to—"

"*Droch sgillinn ort!*" *May an evil shilling find you!* Ceana declared.

Aunt Marta raised her hands over her lips, and Sorcha gasped.

"Aye, Aunt Marta. I hold the amulet that cursed Sorcha." Ceana thundered out the door and down the hall as Anna followed in her wake.

"Ceana, wait!" Anna grabbed her sister's arm to slow her pace. "Please stop and talk to me."

Ceana didn't pause until they reached the bottom

of the stairs to the great hall. A score of men and women were now gathered at the tables for the meal. Ceana was so furious that she didn't even notice Uncle John studying her from the dais.

"Ceana?"

"I have put up with our cousin's wicked behavior long enough. Did ye see, Anna? Did ye see? She threw Mother's pendant on the floor as if it meant naught. Naught! 'Tis bad enough Uncle John had Mother and Father's belongings removed from *our* home and their portraits taken from the verra walls on which they hung, but I will nae have our mother's memory thrown away and banished from thought."

"Shhh…lower your voice. I know how much Mother's pendant means to ye."

A hand clasped down on Ceana's shoulder. "And why are my nieces so distraught, pray tell?"

Ceana turned. Her uncle stood a head taller than she was, and even though he was five years younger than her father, the resemblance was discomforting. Uncle John's dark hair was full with graying strands, and she could see her father's eyes in his. But where her father's eyes had held warmth, Uncle John's did not. He wore the Gunn plaid of blue, green, and red, and affixed at his shoulder was the clan badge—her father's badge—which read "*Aut pax aut bellum.*" *Either peace or war.*

"Uncle John, I—"

"Aye, Cousin. Do tell Father the truth of how ye stole my gown and then cursed me in my own home."

Sorcha, the dragon, made a grand entrance as she descended the stairs with Aunt Marta nipping at her heels.

Ceana's anger and hurt could no longer be controlled. "Och, I'm certain 'tisnae the first time ye've been cur—"

Anna stepped on Ceana's foot at the same time Sorcha's lady maid walked into the great hall, carrying Sorcha's gown. The way the girl quivered in Sorcha's presence incensed Ceana even more.

"Please accept my apologies. The maids told me ye were looking for your lovely dress. After I helped ye remove it last eve, I noticed a small tear in the shoulder. I took your dress to mend it. I had hoped to replace it before... I'm sorry."

"There, there, Beitris," said Aunt Marta. "All is well."

Uncle John chuckled. "I'll leave ye ladies to your dresses."

"Take the gown back to Sorcha's chamber, Beitris."

"Aye, m'lady."

Aunt Marta turned, giving Sorcha a half-scolding look. "Sorcha, donna ye have something to say to Ceana?"

Sorcha brushed Ceana's arm as she passed. "Aye, we're going to be late for the meal."

"My Sorcha has always been a willful child. Ceana, my dear, could ye please find it in your heart to remove the curse ye placed on her? She is looking for a husband, ye know. I'm certain ye were angry, but I know ye donna wish your cousin ill." When Ceana didn't respond, Aunt Marta lowered her voice. "I will have her clean the mess she made in your bedchamber."

"Nay." Ceana didn't need her cousin setting foot in her room again. "I'll do it. And I already removed the curse, Aunt Marta. Sorcha is free to find her husband and start a new life far away from here."

"I'm verra proud to call ye my sister." Anna smiled from ear to ear. "And I thought Aunt Marta was the witch in the clan."

Sitting in the ladies' solar with her sister, Ceana placed her embroidery to the side. She needed a moment to think about how to broach the subject of Samuel. When she gazed around the room and noticed Aunt Marta's more recent touch, she shook her head. "I suppose our cousin didnae see her future husband when she washed her sleeve after all. Aunt Marta has added something new for Sorcha's luck." She nodded to the table.

"The heather?"

"The *white* heather."

Anna lifted a brow. "Why would she do that? Ye told her ye lifted the curse."

"Malvina."

"Pardon?"

Ceana studied her sister thoughtfully for a

moment. "Ye donna remember Mother telling us the tale of Malvina?"

"If Mother told us, I'd love to hear the story again." Anna sat forward in the chair with her hands on her knees. "Tell me."

"According to legend, Ossian, the famous bard, told a tale of Toscar's daughter, Malvina. Now Malvina was the bonniest lass in all the land. It wasnae long before she fell in love and captured the heart of a strong Scottish warrior named Oscar. The two of them became betrothed. In order to provide for his future bride, Oscar took his leave in search of coin to fill the coffers. But as time passed, Malvina missed him dearly."

Ceana continued. "One day she was sitting with Ossian in the Highlands talking about the love of her life, her Oscar, when a man staggered toward them across the moors. Ye see…the man was a messenger who had been sent by Oscar. He told Malvina that her beloved Oscar has been killed in battle, and then the man handed her a spray of purple heather. The heather was a final gift from Oscar, who pledged his undying love for her with his verra last breath."

"That's tragic. What became of her?"

"Malvina was inconsolable when she learned that Oscar had passed. She ran across the moors and through the glen, weeping bitterly. When her tears fell on the ground beneath her feet, the heather turned pure white. When she saw this, she dropped to her knees and prayed that others might ne'er be as unfortunate as her. The white heather is said to be a token of good luck and fortune to those who find it and pluck it. I'm nae surprised Aunt Marta has gathered some for her dear Sorcha."

Anna's expression was grim. "Malvina loved him."

"Aye. We need to talk about Samuel."

"I was wondering how long it would take for ye to broach the subject." Anna glanced at the door and then lowered her voice. "I told Samuel that ye found out about us. He wants to speak with ye but nae in the castle. Can ye meet him at the loch in the morn after ye break your fast?"

"Aye." When the memory of the MacKay guard came to mind, Ceana pushed back the thought. She'd be certain to remain on her father's lands from now on. "Please tell me Raonull, the rogue, doesnae know of your trysts. The man boasts of his conquests to anyone who will listen, and he has a loose tongue. Ye donna want the entire clan knowing about ye and Samuel."

"I asked Samuel nae to tell his brother. He gave his word that he wouldnae. I trust him, as should ye."

"With our parents nay longer here, 'tis my duty to protect ye and do what's best for ye. Samuel is courting my sister. I'll be sure to give him the same courtesy our father would've given him."

"Aye, that's what I'm afraid of."

Ceana wasn't thrilled to be meeting the man who was courting her sister, but she had given her word that she would speak to him. She tied off her mount to a tree and sat on a rock at the loch's edge the next morning. The water lapped gently against the shore and two big birds, perhaps hawks, flew into a branch not far overhead.

"Thank ye for meeting me."

Ceana rose as Samuel approached her. He wore a loose tunic over the Gunn kilt, and a plaid hung over his shoulder. His wavy, reddish-brown hair touched the top of his shoulders, and she noticed his dimples when he smiled. From his boyish good looks, she could see why Anna favored him.

He gestured toward the rock and sat beside her. "Please, sit."

"I've come to understand that ye've been courting my sister."

"Aye, your sister is a fine lass."

"And what exactly are your intentions with Anna?"

His face reddened. "I can assure ye that I have the utmost respect for her. I enjoy our talks. She's witty and makes me laugh. I donna know what the future holds for us, but I..." He lowered his gaze to the ground. "I love her. Ye are her sister. She wants your blessing."

"Your brother—"

"Is a daft fool. I donna listen to his words, nor do I take his advice. I gave my vow to Anna. He doesnae know anything as long as ye donna want him to."

"My sister is all I have left in this world. If ye cause her harm, I will kill ye."

When he noticed the playful expression on her face, he returned her smile. "I understand. Your father was a good man, and he's sorely missed."

"Thank ye."

They sat silently for a long time, and then he rose in one fluid motion.

"Do I have your blessing to court your sister?"

Ceana studied him for a moment. "And why is it that ye're nae asking my uncle for such permission?"

He lifted a brow and gave her a knowing look.

"Aye, as long as my sister wants ye in her life, ye are welcome in mine."

"Thank ye."

"Samuel, how long have ye been in my uncle's guard?"

"I turned eighteen a fortnight ago so I've been with your uncle for nearly two years. I'm sorry to say that I ne'er had the honor of serving your father."

"I see."

He gestured Ceana toward the mounts. "Should we return together, Mistress Gunn?"

"If ye're courting my sister, ye may call me Ceana when we're alone. I'll remain here for a while longer."

"Having your blessing means a lot to us both."

As she watched Samuel, she noticed that even his walk had a sunny cheeriness. He mounted his horse and rode off. She had to admit, she couldn't stay her smile that broadened with approval. When a large shadow loomed over her head, she gazed above her. Three birds were perched on a thick branch—close, almost too close. Perhaps they had a nest somewhere high up in the tree.

"And we meet again, lass. Tell me, what are the odds?"

CHAPTER FOUR

Ceana's eyes darted back and forth. She knew Samuel had already taken his leave, but it was worth trying to look for him in the hope that he could rescue her. With no other choice, she gazed at the man who stood there tall and straight like a towering pine. Oh yes. He was without a doubt the same guard she'd met at the standing stones.

He wore the MacKay plaid of blue, green, and black, and her eyes froze on his long, lean form. She tried not to pay any heed to the large broadsword that was sheathed at his waist. When she looked up at his powerful shoulders, she saw they were covered in leather. He was devilishly handsome. She was surprised she didn't remember that from their first encounter, but she'd been trying to escape his daunting presence at the time. The shadow of his beard gave him a more manly air, and his emerald eyes were startling against his fair skin and light-brown shoulder-length hair.

"What are ye doing here?"

He gestured toward the tree. "I came to fetch my birds."

"The hawks are yours?"

He walked around her. "Aye. They've been with me for quite a while."

"They're beautiful. I can sometimes see them from the parapet flying in the distance, usually killing some poor animal," she said with heavy sarcasm. "Ye better gather them before your men come to find ye."

"Nay one comes out here by the loch or *na tursachan*, but I'm sure ye already know that. 'Tis why ye're here."

"Ye best be on your way."

"I will nae cause ye any harm, but I'll do as ye ask." He held his arms up in the air. "*Trobhadaidh.*" *Come.*

Ceana stood in awe as three hawks flew out of the tree and flocked toward the MacKay man. Two of the birds landed on his shoulders and the other on his arm. "Magnificent."

He gave her a warm smile. "Would ye like to touch one?"

"May I?"

"Aye. Come slowly toward me, and keep your hands and arms down at your side. Donna make any sudden movements."

Ceana walked at a leisurely pace and stopped beside him. "I've ne'er seen one this close before. Do they have names?"

"Aye." He lifted his left shoulder. "This one is

Mac na Bracha." *The son of the malt.* He lifted his right shoulder. "This one is Mac na Praisich." *The son of the still.* "And this one," he raised his arm, "is Mac na Diobhail." *Son of the Devil.*

Ceana bit her lip to stifle a grin.

"I call him that because he bites. The other two recognize the hand that feeds them. Ye may touch the one on my shoulder if ye wish."

"Are ye certain?"

"Aye, that one doesnae bite."

Her raised fingers caressed the soft feathers of the hawk. She couldn't believe she was touching a bird of prey, let alone that the man before her held three. "How do they know to come to ye when ye call for them?"

"Many hours of training and cursing."

She was startled when a laugh escaped her. "Thank ye, truly."

"'Tis my pleasure, lass."

When she realized she didn't know this man at all and was consorting with the enemy alone, she pulled her drifting thoughts together. "Ye best take your leave before—"

"Now why did ye have to do that? We were getting along so well." He cast a roguish grin. "Besides, I cannae yet take my leave. Ye havenae gifted me with your name. What am I to call ye? I am Luthais MacKay."

"If my father's men find ye here—"

"Ah…Mistress Gunn. 'Tis a pleasure to make your

acquaintance." He looked directly at her, and she suddenly felt light-headed. "Tell me. What were ye doing on MacKay lands?"

To her annoyance, she found herself starting to blush. "I was reading my journal."

"But ye could have read your journal here on your own lands. Why were ye on the MacKay's?" When he saw her hesitation, he added, "What do ye think I'm going to do with your answer, lass? 'Tis but a simple question I've asked of ye."

She took another moment, trying to weigh her response. Perhaps a bit of the truth wouldn't be harmful—at least, she hoped not. "As of late, we've had many visitors and I needed a respite, a change of view."

"Too many suitors storming the gates, eh?"

At the remembrance of Sorcha's line of men, Ceana's voice was hoarse with frustration. "Ye have nay idea."

"Och, aye. I understand now. Ye were at the stones to find your husband."

She looked at the man like he had three heads. "Pardon?"

"Come now. Ye must know the tale. Everyone does." His eyes grew amused when he realized she had no idea what he was talking about. "'Tis said that if a man and a woman touch *na tursachan* at the same time and share a kiss, they are destined to be husband and wife."

"And who says that exactly?"

"My clan."

"I see." Her response held a note of impatience. "Most of my clan think the stones have healing properties, while others believe the stones are the home of the fae."

"And what do ye believe?"

"None of it." Without warning, Mac na Diobhail pecked her and she jerked her arm away.

"*Na dean sin!*" *Don't do that!* "Are ye all right?"

Pain shot through her flesh, and she pulled up the sleeve on her dress. Blood was trickling from a small wound on her forearm. "He bit through my dress."

"*Dèan às!*" *Be gone!* As the birds flew away, a feather caught in the wind and floated to the ground. "Please accept my apologies." He pulled a piece of cloth out of his sporran and applied it to her bleeding arm. "I told ye his name suits him." After a few moments, he lifted the material and ran his finger gently over the wound. "The bleeding has stopped."

The mere touch of his hand made Ceana's skin tingle, and she was suddenly conscious of where his warm flesh touched hers. The pain in her arm had turned to a dull ache, and all she was aware of was her racing heart. She was also having a difficult time catching her breath. That was the instant she knew she needed to return home.

The hawk had made her ill.

She pulled her arm from his grasp and took a step away. "Pray excuse me. I'm nae feeling verra well."

"Please, sit down so ye donna fall."

"I only need to rest." She was starting to walk away from the loch when he ran to catch up with her.

"Wait! Then let me escort ye home. 'Twas Mac na Diobhail's fault. The least I can do is make sure ye arrive safely."

"I donna think that's wise." She increased her pace. "My clan will wonder what I'm doing with a MacKay man, and I donna believe they'll give ye time for an explanation if they see ye accompanying me to the gates."

"Let me worry about that."

"And that's why 'tisnae verra wise." She stopped, and when he glanced down, she saw that her fingers were resting on his broad chest. She removed her hand as quickly as if it was on fire.

He briefly gazed away from her and then captured her eyes with his. "Then meet me on the morrow."

"Pardon?"

"I need to know ye are well. I'll meet ye here in the morn after ye break your fast."

"Mister MacKay, let me assure ye that's nae necessary."

"I insist." The man gave her no room for debate. When he saw her thinking of ways to dissuade him, he added, "Then let me say this in a way ye'll understand. If ye donna come on the morrow, I *will* find ye whether ye allow it or nae." By the look on his face, she knew he wasn't jesting.

"Ye're a stubborn man."

"So I've been told."

Against her better judgment, she reluctantly agreed. "Only for ye to see that I am well."

"'Tis all that I ask."

"*Mar sin leat.*" *Good-bye.* Ceana mounted her horse, but instead of fleeing into the safe cover of the forest as she had done the first time, she waited. For what, she wasn't certain. Her mind was telling her to run, but her heart was being foolish and telling her to stay. He placed his hand on the flank of her mount, and when he looked up at her, she felt a strange tingling in the pit of her stomach.

"I'll see ye on the morrow. And again, please accept my apologies."

Luthais couldn't believe Mac na Diobhail had pecked the lass. Perhaps Doughall was right and he needed to spend more time training his hawks. But he'd been taken aback when Mistress Gunn showed an interest in his birds because most of the lasses he knew ran at the sight of them.

Laird Gunn's daughter was a beautiful woman. No wonder she had so many suitors lining up at the gates. But Luthais wasn't foolish. He didn't believe in fate. Life was what you made it. He entered the bailey and released his horse to the stable hand.

"Out finding a wife so soon, or were ye deciding which path to take in order to flee?" asked Doughall with a wide grin.

"Donna worry about me. *'N aire ort fhèin!*" *Look*

after yourself!

His friend's eyes narrowed. "Where were ye?"

"Why? So ye can stalk me for more of my whisky?"

Doughall grabbed the material that hung from Luthais' sporran. "Nay…because I want to know what happened to ye." He held up the soiled cloth.

"'Tisnae my blood."

"Whose blood is it?"

Luthais gave him a firm look of warning and turned, walking into the great hall without his prying friend. The clan sat at the tables because it was already time for the noon meal. Luthais was surprised that so much time had passed while he was with Laird Gunn's daughter. His father stood at the stone fireplace, which wasn't lit, with his hand on the mantel. He looked deep in thought, and Luthais prayed those ideas weren't about him. When they had taken their seats on the dais, his father gazed at him over the rim of his tankard.

"Where did ye ride this morn?"

"To the loch."

"Mmm…I would think ye'd be spending your time making a decision on which lass ye will take to wife. Unless I am mistaken, I donna think being with your birds will give ye an answer to that."

If Luthais had even a spark of hope that his father had been jesting about shackling him to a woman, it was snuffed out like a candle in the rain. But he didn't need his sire plaguing him about finding a wife at every turn. Perhaps he could satisfy the man with a bit of the truth, and then his father wouldn't find it necessary to lecture him.

"I stumbled upon Laird Gunn's daughter at the loch."

His father's eyes lit up. "Ye did?"

"Aye. She's a bonny lass, but ye need to give me time to choose."

Sitting back in the chair, his father studied him. "Ye surprise me, Luthais. I'm proud to see ye considering this matter seriously. Ye do realize that making an alliance with the Gunns would be in the best interest of the clan. Although the choice is yours, I hope ye choose wisely."

"I can assure ye, Father, that I am giving Mistress Gunn the attention she deserves."

"I donna want to wed him, Father. The man is verra sore on the eyes."

Ceana felt pain in her shin as Anna kicked her under the table.

Uncle John set down his tankard, tapping his finger on the rim. "Ye donna have to wed him, but ye must marry one of these men, Sorcha. A marriage to any of them would form an alliance with our clan."

Anna's eyes lit up as Samuel sat at one of the tables in front of the dais. When he saw Anna watching him, his expression mirrored that of her sister, and Ceana tried to stay her smile.

"What do ye think, Ceana? Which one of these men should I choose?" Resting her chin in the palm of her hand, Sorcha waited for an answer.

Ceana wasn't a fool and knew her cousin's words were meant to cut like a knife. Refusing to be baited into another heated argument, Ceana pasted a bright smile on her face. "With so many suitors, your decision must be a difficult one. But if I were ye, I'd wed the one whose lands are the farthest distance away."

"I donna know if that's the best way to choose your husband," said Aunt Marta. "Perhaps ye should try washing your sleeve again this eve, my dear."

"Please, nay more apparitions, Aunt Marta," said Anna.

"Mayhap I'm nae thinking of this clearly. More than likely I should choose a man who's much closer to home. Who wouldnae want a man like Samuel who isnae sore on the eyes?" All color drained from Anna's face, and Sorcha's eyes lit up. "What do ye think, Anna?"

"What do I think? I think that ye're—"

"Daughter, your jesting doesnae make anyone laugh. The boy may be fair of face, but he isnae suitable for marriage, especially to my daughter."

Sorcha waved her father off. "I know, Father. I have many men to consider, but I do thank ye for giving me a choice."

Uncle John rose. "I must see to the rents. Pray excuse me."

When a smug look crossed her cousin's face, Ceana wanted to be the one to wipe it clean. In lieu of throttling Sorcha where she sat, Ceana leaned in close and lifted a brow. She was careful to speak with an air of indifference. "Ye know, Sorcha... If ye donna want to choose a husband whose lands are far away, and ye donna want to wash your sleeve again, mayhap ye should ask yourself which man would show ye the most tolerance. That's the one I would choose if I were ye."

CHAPTER FIVE

Luthais donned his kilt and tunic, pulled on his boots, and didn't even bother to break his fast. He'd slept longer than expected because all he did was toss and turn into the early hours of the morn. His responsibilities were weighing heavily on his mind. Granted, he wanted to make his father proud, but he had a very hard time preventing a certain woman from invading his thoughts.

As he made his way toward the stables, he wondered if Mistress Gunn would be foolish enough to break her word. He silently prayed she wouldn't and no longer wanted to dwell on the reasons why. As he rode through the village, he didn't see the blacksmith who had raised his hand in greeting. Hell, he didn't even notice that Doughall was trailing after him when he rode through the glen. Luthais' mind was muddled, which usually got him into trouble.

As he passed the standing stones, he gazed into the stone circle and found it empty. Not that he had expected Mistress Gunn to return. But the memory of her sitting against the giant rock with her nose buried in her journal and not a care in the world made his heart skip a beat. And the way the sun had shone down on her chestnut locks made him think that perhaps the tales were true. She was delivered by the fae.

Luthais approached the edge of the loch and tied off his mount. The only movement came from the blades of grass and the leaves that rustled in the gentle wind. He sat on a rock, watching the water lap onto the pebble shore. He'd wait and give the lass a few moments before he decided to do anything rash like pound on the Gunns' gates to see her.

"Mister MacKay, I didnae recognize ye without your birds."

He rose, and his eyes narrowed. "Do ye know 'tisnae wise to sneak up on a man? I could verra well have run my sword through ye."

Mistress Gunn glanced at the broadsword sheathed at his waist. "To be truthful, that was the furthest thought from my mind. I was more worried about Mac na Diobhail pecking me again. Pray tell, where is that dastardly bird?" She glanced over her shoulder at the tree behind her.

"I havenae yet seen any of them this morn."

"More than likely for the best. They're out stalking some poor animal for sure."

He gave her a patient smile. "I see ye are well."

"I was well when we last parted, Mister MacKay. Ye didnae need to worry over me."

He shrugged with indifference. "I needed to see with my own eyes. I will nae offer apologies for seeing to your welfare." When she averted his gaze, he added, "Now that ye're here, would ye like to sit and enjoy the view with me?" She flushed, and he turned up his smile a notch.

"Mister MacKay, ye know that's nae verra appropriate."

"I believe the time for propriety passed when ye set foot on MacKay lands." When he lifted a brow in a jesting manner, she folded her hands in front of her and smiled. They exchanged a subtle look of amusement.

"Be that as it may, I—"

"Mistress Gunn, I assure ye my intentions are honorable." He paid no heed to the mocking voice inside his head—the same voice that wondered why he hadn't left all of his noble intentions at home.

Ceana hesitated as she fought to clear the cobwebs in her mind. From her brief experience with the man, she could tell that he was stubborn enough to seek her out even if she hadn't come to the loch. But he could see that she was well. What could he want from her now? What frightened her even more was the fact that she wanted to find out.

"Come now and sit. Only Mac na Diobhail bites."

She didn't think that was entirely true. Once again, against her better judgment, she ambled toward him when she should've turned around and fled. "I will stay for a moment." She sat on the rock beside him and straightened her skirts. When there was a moment of silence, she studied him as he gazed out at the loch. There was an air of solitude about him, yet, she felt something vaguely familiar. Perhaps she sensed a kindred spirit.

"I havenae seen rain upon us for a few days now. There isnae a cloud in the sky. Mayhap this is a sign we will nae have another harsh Highland winter."

She found that her mood was suddenly becoming buoyant. "I cannae say that I ever remember nae having a harsh winter."

"There is truth in that." He briefly paused. "May I ask what ye were so engrossed in reading at *na tursachan* the other day?"

She waved her hand in a dismissive gesture. "Oh, 'twas naught that exhilarating, only my journal. I write my thoughts."

"I admire a woman who educates her mind." He cast a smile that warmed her heart. "Ye know? I've lived here all my life, but I'm certain that I've ne'er seen ye before. Why is that?"

"My mother and father didnae make a habit of taking me and my sister out from the protection of our lands."

He lifted a brow. "I didnae know ye had a sister. Should I let the guards know that we should be expecting to find her at *na tursachan* as well?"

Ceana boldly met his eyes as his gaze froze on her

lips. "That's nae necessary. Ye would ne'er find her on your lands with a book in hand because my sister has an aptness for avoiding her studies. Furthermore, I can assure ye, Mister MacKay, that nae all Gunn women are the same. Believe me."

"I should hope nae." His voice became soft and alluring. "Tell me, Mistress Gunn. With all the suitors coming to your gates, have ye chosen one, or even found a man to your liking?"

"*Me?*" She placed her hand to her chest and couldn't stay the laugh that escaped her. "Nay. Why do ye ask?" She was glad she was sitting because the way the man smiled at her made her knees tremble.

"If ye must know, the thought pleases me."

When his eyes darkened with some unidentifiable emotion, Ceana didn't know what to do. Was this man—and a MacKay man at that—showing an interest in her and not Princess Sorcha? Perhaps her imagination was getting the best of her and she was secretly hoping for something that wasn't there. The idea came to mind when without warning, he leaned slightly in to her, tilting his handsome face toward hers.

"I'm going to kiss ye now. Donna be afraid."

She could hear her own breath becoming ragged. "I am nae afraid." Deep down she was petrified.

He moved his mouth over hers, and the touch of his lips was tender and passionate. The kiss was slow and thoughtful, as if he wanted her to savor every delicious moment. Her heart jolted and her pulse pounded. God help her because she was powerless to resist him. His fingers caressed her cheek, her flesh prickling at his mere touch. She was shocked at her own eager response. She knew she should deny him, but she couldn't.

When he forced her lips open with his thrusting tongue, she was hesitant at first, clumsy in her actions. No man had ever touched her that way. And why was she letting this MacKay man be the first? She had no idea. But she really didn't care because this had to be a sin to feel so right.

The world ceased to exist.

She was not a Gunn, and he was not a MacKay. They were man and woman. Her thoughts spun. Her emotions whirled, but it wasn't long before she was returning his kiss with reckless abandon, matching the thrusting and parrying of his tongue in her mouth. Her hands slid up his brawny arms to his wide, leather-strapped shoulders. She pulled her hand away when her fingers brushed a talon. She wasn't surprised she hadn't heard or seen the hawk. Frankly, the two of them could've been under siege and she wouldn't have noticed.

Raising his mouth from hers, he gazed into her eyes and gently rubbed his thumb along her jaw. "Thank ye for that."

"Am I supposed to say 'Ye're welcome' in response?" Ceana knew he was trying to stay a chuckle, but one escaped him anyway. "I see we have a visitor." She nodded to his shoulder.

"Ye arenae afraid?"

Since she wasn't certain if he was asking whether she was frightened of him or his hawk, she shook her head. "I recognize the hawk isnae the Son of the Devil. Please donna misunderstand me. I'm nae afraid of Mac na Diobhail, but I donna want another bite on my arm."

"From someone who has had his fair share of pecks from the wee bastard…er, bird, I understand how ye feel and cannae say that I blame ye." The hawk moved down the leather strap on Luthais's arm and flew away into the air. "Hmm…Mac na Bracha found something more interesting than me."

Ceana couldn't imagine what. Without warning, she caught a figure rushing toward them out of the corner of her eye.

Luthais unsheathed his weapon when the young man charged him. The sound of scraping swords not only ended the private moment with Mistress Gunn, but also made Luthais irked by this whelp's intrusion. The Gunn plaid hung over the man's shoulder, and his wavy, reddish-brown hair touched the top of his shoulders.

"Samuel! Put away your sword! Now!"

The man's eyes widened, but Luthais wasn't foolish enough to lower his weapon. He could easily bring the boy to his knees, but if the lad called for the guards, the last Luthais's father needed was to come and rescue his son from the Gunn dungeon. Luthais would make certain it wouldn't come to that.

"I suggest ye do what the lass says before ye get hurt, laddie." When Mistress Gunn inched closer and the man moved his sword in a nervous gesture, Luthais added, "Or ye might injure the lass."

"I was searching for ye and saw ye with him." The man was stammering and had a puzzled expression on his face.

"Samuel, ye see that I am well. Lower your sword. Mister MacKay will nae harm either one of us."

When she gave Luthais an imploring look to confirm her words, he put the matter aside with sudden good humor. "I'm nae really in the mood for swordplay, lad." He sheathed his sword as the young man hesitantly did the same.

"Samuel, this is Mister MacKay." She turned to Luthais. "Samuel courts my sister." She smiled as though her words explained everything.

"I see."

"The laird is requesting your presence at the castle."

"Of course. Thank ye for seeing to my welfare, Mister MacKay. Mayhap I'll see ye and your birds again in the morn sometime soon." She looked at him hopefully, and he gave her a slight bow.

"It would be an honor. Ye'd best nae keep your father waiting."

"Oh, he's nae my fa—"

"Luthais!"

He looked over his shoulder to see the mighty Doughall sitting on his steed a couple stone throws away. "Do ye need my aid?"

"Do I need your...*what?* Nay!" When Luthais turned around, he tried to mask the look of disgust that crossed his face. Sometimes Doughall was as vexing as his birds.

Mistress Gunn gazed up at him with an effort. She placed her hand at the base of her throat, and her eyes darted back to Doughall. "Who is that?" Her voice went up a notch.

"I think we need to make haste," said Samuel.

"I think that's a good idea. It was a pleasure to see ye again, Mister MacKay. I assume that ye'll take your birds with ye." She looked back at Doughall. "And your man."

Before Luthais could say anything, she walked away with the young guard. Not only was Luthais unhappy with the intrusion of the young Gunn guard, but now he also was angry with his friend. Curses fell from Luthais's mouth as he untied his mount from the tree and made his way over to Doughall. The bastard shifted his weight in the saddle, couldn't look him in the eye, and didn't utter a single word about his purpose for being there.

Luthais swung his leg over his mount and refused to wipe the scowl from his face. "Now ye're following me?"

"I think it best if we have this conversation on MacKay lands."

They rode side by side, neither one of them taking the time to look at the other. Luthais clenched his mouth tighter so he wouldn't say anything he'd regret. All he'd wanted was some time alone with Mistress Gunn, and his purpose had quickly gone awry. He'd seen the look on her face. How could he miss it? She'd had the same expression as most lasses. Doughall frightened men on the battlefield with his fierce looks alone.

As soon as they reached MacKay lands, Luthais blurted out, "I want to know why in the hell ye were following me."

"Since ye wouldnae tell me what ye've been up to, ye left me nay choice. I wanted to be certain ye werenae doing anything foolish like with rope, sheep, and lovers. But I see that I'm too late. Ye took the innocence of the laird's daughter."

Luthais glowered at his friend and raised his voice so that Doughall wouldn't miss a single word. "I didnae take her innocence, ye damn fool!"

"I've seen the blood, remember?"

When Doughall gave him an impatient look, Luthais continued. He hadn't noticed the strained tone in his voice. "I met her acquaintance at *na tursachan* and saw her again at the loch where Mac na Diobhail pecked her arm. I wanted to see if she was all right. That was the blood ye saw."

"Wait a moment. Let me get this right in my head. Ye showed the lass your birds?" Doughall stared at him and then burst out laughing. "So ye let her pet your hawks and nae your cock?"

Luthais reined in his mount and gave Doughall a swift punch in the arm. The man didn't even flinch. "Bastard."

"Ye should have had me come along, Luthais. I could have showed ye the proper way to woo a lass."

"Ye know damn well that the lasses run at the sight of ye. And I'll have ye know that I was doing just fine until ye and the whelp came alone and interrupted us. Now that ye know the truth, I nay longer want ye following me. I donna need your assistance. Do ye understand?"

"I wasnae following ye—well, I was, but I was coming to warn ye as your friend."

"Warn me? About what?"

"Your father. *A bheil fhios agad?*" *Do you know?* "He's found ye a bride."

Luthais stopped his mount, and suddenly everything around him became very still. He could hear his own blood pumping in his ears. "*Chan eil mi a 'tuigsinn.*" *I don't understand.*

"I wouldnae be too upset if I were ye, especially since it seems ye already favor the lass."

Luthais rubbed his hand over his brow. "What the hell did he do?"

"Your father sent a messenger to Laird Gunn this morn. He offered your hand in marriage to the Gunn's daughter and an alliance with the clan."

CHAPTER SIX

As soon as the stable hand took their mounts, Ceana pulled Samuel through the bustling courtyard. Having him open his mouth to her uncle, her aunt, her cousin, or even her sister would not bode well for her, especially after lecturing Anna about Samuel and their secret trysts. Frankly, she'd never hear the end of it.

"Nae a single word. Do ye understand?"

"What were ye doing with that MacKay man? And what was he doing on our lands?"

She stopped before the entrance to the great hall. "That is nay concern of yours, but if ye must know, I was the one who trespassed on his lands." Welcoming Samuel's confusion, Ceana took a moment to catch her breath.

"But why?"

That was indeed the question. "I needed a respite from my cousin and my aunt."

He chuckled. "Ye donna need to tell me twice. I'm nae sure how ye and Anna manage to put up with the lot of them. They'd drive me mad. But that doesnae explain why ye entered MacKay territory without an escort. That could've been verra dangerous, a lass alone."

"I traveled to the standing stones."

Samuel's eyes lit up as if he held a secret. "Ah, I understand now what ye were doing. Ye were seeking a husband. Anna and I have talked about *na tursachan* many times. Ye know the tales. Your sister has asked me to take her before, but I'm nae foolish enough to travel onto the MacKay's lands."

Ceana squeezed her fingers over the bridge of her nose. "I was hoping to hear ye say that ye arenae foolish enough to believe the tales, but the fact that ye and my sister are even thinking about marriage frightens me. I'm letting ye court my sister. Give me your word that ye will nae tell anyone what ye saw, especially Anna." Ceana shifted from foot to foot. "What did ye see anyway?"

His eyes grew amused. "I didnae witness ye lock lips with the MacKay man, if that's what ye're asking." When he winked at her, she slapped him playfully on the arm.

"Samuel…"

"Ye can trust me."

She hoped that was true. Needing to change the subject, she displayed an ease that she didn't necessarily feel. After all, she wasn't overjoyed to be speaking about such a private matter with Samuel. "Do ye know what my uncle wanted?"

"He asked to see ye and Anna after a messenger arrived this morn."

A deep voice spoke from behind her. "Is my brother troubling ye?"

She whipped her head around to find Raonull standing there with observant eyes and his hands placed on his lean hips. This was just what she needed—the loosest tongue and the biggest rogue of the castle involved in her private matters.

He was tall, rawboned, and beardless, with an ingenuously appealing face. His hair was the color of field oats, and his skin was pulled taut over the elegant ridge of his cheekbones. She could almost see why women flaunted themselves at him in a discomfiting way. Almost. The way he stood there told everyone that he knew he was handsome, and that irked her even more. No one should be that beautiful. Thankfully, she and Anna were not among the many foolish women who had shared Raonull's bed. Although the rogue was indeed a rougher version of Samuel, he lacked Samuel's kindness and compassion.

"Your brother hasnae been troubling me at all."

"Mmm...I'll take certain precautions and make sure that he doesnae." Raonull slapped his hand on Samuel's shoulder. "Come along, Brother."

When the men walked away, Ceana released the breath that she didn't know she held. If she could start the day over, she would, especially its beginning with Luthais at the loch. She brought her fingers to her lips, smiling because she knew she'd always remember her first kiss. A part of her was glad the moment was with Luthais, even though he was a MacKay. He'd made her feel special, something she didn't experience often enough. She turned as Anna was coming out of the great hall.

"Anna!"

"Where have ye been? Uncle John has been looking for ye because he wants to meet with us. I donna think my nerves can handle whatever 'tis he wants to speak with us about. He ne'er wants to talk with us privately behind the closed doors of his study. Do ye think this has something to do with our mother and father? Mayhap they finally found the vagrants who left them for dead on the—"

"Anna, it's been two years. Uncle John couldnae find the men responsible then, and I doubt he's found them now."

They walked into the great hall and stopped dead in their tracks. Three wooden basins were placed in a line on the hearth as Aunt Marta blindfolded Sorcha.

"What are they doing now?" asked Ceana.

"I've seen Aunt Marta do this before," whispered Anna. "One of the bowls is filled with clean water from the well, another with muddy water from the stream, and the last one is empty." Aunt Marta handed Sorcha a stick, and Sorcha pointed to one of the basins. "After each time Sorcha chooses, Aunt Marta will change the position of the bowls. Sorcha has to choose the same one twice before she can stop."

"And what is that supposed to do or tell, or should I even ask?"

"Aunt Marta told me that if Sorcha chooses the basin with the pure water, she'll have an honorable marriage. The choice with the muddy water means marriage in dishonor. And if she chooses the one with no water, she'll ne'er be wed. Should we stay and find out Sorcha's fate?"

Ceana grabbed her sister by the arm. "Come. If Sorcha thinks basins will tell her the future, so be it. But neither ye nor I should be witness to this madness any longer. Let's find out what Uncle John wanted to speak with us about."

"What the hell have ye done?" Luthais ran his fingers through his hair as he paced in front of his father, who sat behind the wooden desk in his study. "I told ye that I met Laird Gunn's daughter. I told ye that I wanted more time. God's teeth! I wanted to see if she'd be suitable as my wife. I wanted to woo her, and ye didnae even give me the chance."

His father chuckled. "Woo her? There's plenty of time for that later...after ye're wed."

"Lest ye forget, that choice was to be my own!"

"Luthais, I told ye that I was proud to see ye considering this matter with the importance ye should, but ye know making an alliance with the Gunns would be in the best interest of the clan, and sooner rather than later. The more I thought about your words, the clearer they became. Your marriage would bring with it powerful allies. The MacKays and Gunns would be a force to be reckoned with. I couldnae let ye foul up our…er, your future." He sat down and rested his arm on the desk.

"And there lies the truth to it all, Father."

"I understand ye may be cross at me for—"

"Cross doesnae even begin to describe how I feel. Ye want me to make decisions for the clan, but how can I do that when ye make them for me at every turn?"

His father stiffened in the chair. "Ye are my son. Ye will learn there are things in life that ye must do even when ye donna want to do them. I must travel to Edinburgh every year, and ye know that isnae something I favor."

"Ye go to Edinburgh because the king orders all the Highland lairds to attend court. I take my vows seriously, Father. Once I say them, there will be nay turning back. The choice was to be mine. The last I needed was my sire forcing me to the altar and choosing my bride. I am a man. Ye need to stop interfering in my life and worry about your own."

His father's mouth twitched with amusement. "And the last time I didnae interfere I believe there was a sheep and rope involved."

Luthais rose to his feet in exasperation. "Is that all ye see? I will nae apologize for thinking that other issues have greater importance than sheep stealing and tupping. I want to know what ye said in the missive."

"I merely told Laird Gunn that if his daughter hasnae chosen a suitor, my son wishes to be among them for consideration. And of course I mentioned that if ye took her to wife, the MacKays and Gunns would become powerful allies."

Luthais couldn't help himself when a growl escaped him. "So ye sealed my fate by a missive. Did ye ever think this would've been better had I approached Laird Gunn himself when I was ready and asked for his daughter's hand in marriage?" When his father didn't respond, Luthais spoke for him. "Of course nae."

"While we wait for Laird Gunn's response, why donna ye spend your time wooing the lass? That is what ye wanted, eh?"

"Donna make light of what ye did. I disagree with everything about this."

His father rose and walked around the desk. "Aye, but ye will do what is expected of ye. Ye are a MacKay. I'd be proud for ye to take my place one day as laird."

"And one day I promise ye that I will. But when will ye realize that we are two different men? We will nae see things the same way, and to think that we could is foolish. Ye are my father, but if ye do anything like that again, I swear that ye may nae live to see the morrow."

Luthais walked to the stables, placing as much

distance between himself and his sire as he possibly could. He loved his father, he truly did, but sometimes he felt like throttling the man. He supposed the feeling was mutual between any father and son. He opened the wooden door to the stables, and the smell of hay engulfed his senses.

"Would ye like me to saddle your mount?" asked one of the stable hands.

"I'm only going to brush him. Thank ye."

Luthais picked up a brush from the bucket on the ground and opened the door to his mount's stall. He swept the brush down the horse's flank while pondering over Mistress Gunn. The kiss with her had stirred something within him that he hadn't felt for a very long time. He wasn't sure what, but he liked talking with her, and he certainly enjoyed touching her. He couldn't help but wonder what she'd say when she found out she might be his wife.

Laird John Gunn gazed at his two nieces sitting across from him in his study. The younger one moved restlessly in her chair with her fingers tensed on her lap, and the older one was studying him intently. The two lasses were barely women and nothing but a necessary thorn in his side. Sorcha had never cared for the girls, and Marta only tolerated them out of respect for his brother.

He realized now that he should've given much more thought to his nieces' existence before he'd taken care of the other pain-in-his-arse and his busybody wife two years ago. But his brother had rarely traveled with the girls. Any scheme would've been difficult to execute on Gunn lands. But now he had to deal with the scraps that remained of his brother's legacy.

"I wanted to meet with ye both to discuss your future. As ye know, Sorcha has had many suitors, and I am trying to arrange a marriage for her. After my daughter is settled with her new husband, I will be making marriages for the both of ye as well."

Anna paled, and Ceana sat forward, placing her hand on the desk. "Uncle John, Anna is but fifteen years old. I donna think we need to rush into—"

His eyes narrowed. "Who do ye think ye are to question my decisions? I am your uncle and your laird. Ye will show me respect." Responding to the tone of his voice, his niece wisely removed her hand from the desk and sat back in the chair. He remembered his brother's wife acting much the same... And then he thought back on how he'd ended her life.

When Ceana saw Anna's pained expression, she had to speak her mind. She knew her sister as well as she knew herself. Anna loved Samuel. The thought of being forced to wed someone else would be her sister's undoing. Ceana needed to make her uncle understand. She had to get him to see reason.

"Uncle John, I recognize how important 'tis for ye to find Sorcha a husband, but Anna isnae yet ready to wed."

His eyes grew amused. "She will wed when I say she's ready to wed."

Her sister's eyes welled with tears. There had to be a way to get their uncle to change his mind, but the only option she could think of was telling the truth. "But Anna loves another."

"Ceana!" Anna's voice was laced with panic.

"What man does she love?" asked Uncle John.

Ceana gave her sister a look of encouragement. "Samuel," whispered Anna. A heaviness centered in Ceana's chest when Uncle John threw back his head and let out a great peal of laughter. Her sister was sobbing beside her.

"Samuel? I just told Sorcha the lad may be fair of face, but nay niece of mine will be marrying him."

Although Ceana was disappointed by her uncle's answer, she felt for the first time as if he cared about his nieces as much as he did his own daughter. "But what if Anna *wanted* to wed—"

"Sorcha will wed the MacKay's son, and my nieces will nae be wed to men who will remain under my roof. I will find ye husbands, and ye will both be living far away from here. Edinburgh mayhap." He stood. "I have more pressing concerns."

He was about to walk out the door when Ceana murmured, "My father's."

Uncle John stopped mid-stride and turned around.

"Pardon?"

"Ye said we will nae remain under your roof. 'Tis my father's roof." Her uncle closed the distance that was left between them and roughly pulled Ceana to her feet. Anna gasped, and Ceana's breath caught in her lungs as her uncle painfully squeezed her arms.

His eyes darkened dangerously. "Ye overstep."

"Uncle, please let go of my sister. I'll wed—"

He released his grip and shoved Ceana away from him. "I've become a greater man than your father was or could ever be." And with that, Uncle John stormed out the door.

Ceana turned, embracing Anna who was weeping aloud. Anna's heart was breaking before Ceana's eyes. Everything suddenly became clear. Her feelings had been right all along. She and Anna meant nothing to anyone since the death of their parents. Sorcha was all that was important in the world. For a moment, Ceana felt pity for Laird MacKay's son. She'd have to ask Luthais what he thought of the man. But since the MacKay's son stood among a long line of Sorcha's waiting suitors, Ceana wouldn't dwell on it any longer.

The man deserved to be left to his own demise for marrying her despicable cousin.

CHAPTER SEVEN

Luthais didn't even bother to ask the stable hand to saddle his mount. He often found that doing tasks himself distracted him from his ever-mounting frustration. All he did was toss and turn throughout the night because the future looked vague and shadowy. He prayed Mistress Gunn wasn't angry with him and hoped she might meet him at the loch this morn. He wanted to explain his father's eagerness in sending the missive to her father.

When the sound of pounding hoofbeats came through the gates, Luthais glanced over his shoulder and hesitated. The man wore a Gunn kilt, and his face was clouded with uneasiness. Luthais supposed he'd feel just as uncomfortable riding into the Gunn bailey alone. As Luthais approached the man, he found that his own palms were starting to sweat, especially since the contents of the message were unknown. But he knew what the subject was and that unsettled him.

"I'm delivering a message to Laird MacKay from the Gunn."

"Give it to me and I will make certain my father gets it. I am Luthais MacKay." He held up his hand.

"There's nay need. I'm here now. I'll take that." His father approached Luthais from behind and took the missive from the man's grasp.

Luthais watched the billowing dust that followed the messenger out the gates as the man fled as quickly as he'd arrived. When Luthais faced his father, the wax seal was already broken and his father was reading the note. His sire was smiling from ear to ear as he slapped the missive into Luthais's hand.

"The Gunn has agreed to discuss the terms of your marriage to his daughter."

Luthais wasn't certain whether he should be terrified or feel relief that Mistress Gunn was to be his bride. "Aye, well, ye have done enough. From now on, I will handle this matter the way I see fit. Do ye understand? Ye arenae to be involved with my decisions. I will make my own."

"Luthais…" His father slapped him on the shoulder. "Ye have found your bride. I couldnae be more proud of ye than I am right now. Ye've done as I asked."

"I'm glad to hear it. Mount up. We ride to Laird Gunn's."

His father looked at him in surprise. "Now?"

"Aye, now. I want to speak with Mistress Gunn. I donna think it wise to fire my future wife's ire before we are even wed. I'm sure I'll be doing enough of that after I am her husband."

Ceana broke her fast although she wanted nothing more than to stay in bed under the blankets and shut out the world beyond her bedchamber door. She'd spent the night on the parapet with Samuel and Anna, trying to convince them not to do anything foolish. After all, Sorcha was not yet wed, and there was still time to figure out what to do. Although Ceana knew her sister was in turmoil over thoughts of not being with Samuel, Ceana couldn't overlook her own feelings. Even from her brief encounters with Luthais, a part of her had started to favor him. The idea of losing his companionship before she even had a chance to know him was not something she was amenable to.

Uncle John was quiet and wisely didn't gaze in Ceana or Anna's direction at the table. Since Aunt Marta and Sorcha were in yet another conversation about the wedding, Ceana made it a point not to listen. She was aware that the celebration would be no small affair because everything with respect to her cousin was extravagant. When she glanced at her sister, she noticed that Anna's shoulders were rounded, her face was grim, and she was playing with the food on the trencher.

Ceana patted Anna's thigh. "'Tis going to be all right. Ye'll see."

Her sister nodded with a bleak expression on her face, and Ceana suddenly longed for her mother and father. How she wished she had some type of magic in her blood and could be transported back in time to the way it was before. What was wrong with her? She was starting to sound like Aunt Marta, of all things. But the truth was that she'd like nothing more than to be able to wipe away all the heartbreak and misery of the past two years.

When the meal was over, she walked through the courtyard to the stable. After her mount was saddled, she rode across the field to the loch as she'd done so many times before. She looked up at the gray skies and didn't see any of Luthais's hawks flying overhead. She hoped that wasn't a sign that he wasn't there to see her, especially after their private moment together.

She cleared the trees and dismounted. With the threat of storm clouds looming above, she hastily walked her horse toward the water's edge. Luthais was nowhere in sight. She sighed, realizing her life had become nothing but a bitter battle of disappointments. Perhaps she'd offended him or done something wrong. She hoped that he realized she didn't let just any man from the neighboring clan kiss her.

There was a loud clap of thunder, and time was running out. As she gazed around the loch one more time, the wind picked up and whipped her long hair into her face. She'd have to try to see him again soon.

Rain was pelting her face when she rode through the gates to the bailey. The stable hand greeted her, grabbing the reins of her horse as she dismounted. She didn't waste any time dashing across the courtyard and into the great hall. As she shook the rain off her cloak, she realized it was yet another lovely day in the Highlands.

Aunt Marta, Sorcha, and Anna stood huddled in a corner. When Ceana approached them, she could hear joy bubbling in Sorcha's laugh as well as shining in her eyes. Her smile even broadened with approval when she saw Ceana.

"Oh, Cousin. I can barely stand it any longer." Sorcha gave Ceana a quick embrace and then released her. "Father is in his study now discussing my dowry with my future husband and his father. I cannae wait to meet him. From what I saw when he arrived, he's verra handsome. Did ye hear? I'm to wed Laird MacKay's son. Father is so proud that my marriage will bring with it an alliance with the MacKays."

"Aye, I've heard. I hope ye two will be verra happy together."

"Thank ye, Ceana. I hope ye mean that. I know we havenae always been friends, but mayhap ye can share this moment with me."

"Ye'll be a lovely bride, Sorcha." No matter how hard Ceana tried, she couldn't forget her cousin's abominable behavior. Anna must have read her sister's thoughts because she rubbed her hand over Ceana's shoulder and gave her an encouraging smile.

A very large, red-haired man entered the great hall from the direction of her uncle's study, and everyone in the room fell silent. The man was at least six and a half feet tall, a giant who looked ready to slaughter anything in his path. He gazed around the room as if he was deciding who to choose for his next victim. Oh, the irony of it all. Perhaps Ceana's days would now be brighter, knowing that Sorcha's venomous behavior would never be tolerated by such a man.

But the more Ceana studied the redheaded beast, the more something unsettled her. He looked vaguely familiar. Was he the same imposing man who had been at the loch? She thought he might be. If so, he was definitely not Laird MacKay's son. He was a guard, the same as Luthais.

Uncle John and an older man with graying hair came into the great hall and spoke for a moment with the redheaded giant. Since the older gentleman wore the same tartan as Luthais, he had to be Laird MacKay. No sooner did she recognize that fact than her heart skipped a beat. Another man walked around the circle of men.

Luthais...

When Luthais and his father left Laird Gunn's study, Luthais knew he'd made his father proud. How could he not? Not only was he able to negotiate his future wife's dowry, but he and his father had made an alliance with the Gunns—something they'd thought would never come to fruition in either of their lifetimes.

He followed the men into the great hall, and Laird Gunn slapped him on the back. "Would ye like to meet my daughter?"

Luthais glanced over his shoulder and saw that the lovely enchantress had already spotted him. Her mouth was slightly parted and her skin was pale. She needn't worry because he wasn't foolish enough to let anyone know of the times they'd met before. He had a strong desire to show her that the two of them would be all right together. In fact, everything was now perfect.

He gave a brief nod to Laird Gunn. "She is the most beautiful lass in the room. Please allow me the honor." Mistress Gunn wore a cloak, and her hair was wet from the rain. He didn't realize he was smiling. Perhaps she'd gone to the loch to find him, but he was here, arranging for her to be his wife. As he closed the distance between them, her eyes widened. He reached out and clutched her hand.

"Chan eil mi a' tuigsinn," she whispered. *I don't understand.*

He gazed into her eyes and brushed a gentle kiss on the top of her hand. Everyone in the room gasped with excitement. "What is there to understand, Mistress Gunn?" He gave her a slight bow. "I am Luthais MacKay, and I am honored to make your acquaintance...as well as have ye for my wife." An unidentifiable expression crossed her face, and tears welled in her eyes. He was about to question her further when some chit with brown, bouncing curls around her face stepped between them.

Luthais stood to his full height, and his eyes narrowed. He was unhappy with the intrusion.

"I am Sorcha Gunn. *I* am the one ye will be marrying. That is my cousin, Ceana."

He took one step to the side and gave the woman he'd met at the loch an imploring look—the same woman with whom he'd shared a stolen kiss, an embrace. An unexplainable heaviness centered in his chest, and as casually as he could manage, Luthais said, "But ye're the laird's daughter."

The bubbly Sorcha stepped between them again. "Ceana isnae the laird's daughter. I am."

Luthais was suddenly flanked by his father and Laird Gunn. "Is there something amiss? This is my lovely daughter, Sorcha."

When Luthais didn't respond, his father spoke for him. "Ye cannae blame the lad. He's only taken with your daughter's beauty and finds himself at a loss for words."

Luthais shared a smile with Sorcha as he felt bile rise in the back of his throat. All eyes were on him. He needed to do something fast. Until he could figure out what the hell this was about, he had to play along with another bad situation he'd gotten himself into or they'd all be warring in the great hall. Sorcha lifted her hand, and with no choice, he kissed the top of it just as he saw Mistress Gunn—Ceana—walk away out of the corner of his eye.

"'Tis a pleasure to make your acquaintance." He

felt the air in the great hall lighten when he acknowledged his true betrothed and knew he had to get out of there. He turned to her father. "Laird Gunn, if ye'll pray excuse us, we have another important matter to attend to."

"Of course. I'll make certain everything is in order here so that ye and my daughter can be wed within the fortnight."

Luthais nodded. "Verra well. And Mistress Gunn…until we meet again."

"Mayhap ye can pay me another visit before the wedding? I'd love to see ye again."

He gave her an appeasing smile and walked briskly toward Doughall. He hoped his father followed because he wasn't waiting for him to catch up. Luthais was breathless with rage. His expression was thunderous. He could hear the blood pounding in his ears. He entered the bailey throwing curses under his breath like stones. He raked his fingers through his hair as the stable hand brought their mounts. Thankfully, his father and Doughall were wise enough not to open their mouths.

The men mounted and rode through the gates, their horses flinging mud behind them from the rain. It wasn't long before Luthais once again found himself flanked.

"What the hell was that all about? Ye said ye already met the Gunn's daughter," said his father.

"The woman wasnae the same lass Luthais had met," said Doughall.

His father's voice went up a notch. "What do ye mean she wasnae the same lass?"

"She wasnae the same lass!" Luthais bellowed. "I've been played for a damn fool."

"I think we should—"

Luthais shot his father a cold look. "*We* will do naught. I donna want to hear another word. I will handle this mess."

He had no idea how, but he had a pretty good idea where to start.

Ceana stood in her bedchamber and held her mother's pendant close to her heart. Dear God. How could she not have known Luthais was the MacKay's son? This whole time she assumed he was a guard. The nagging in her mind refused to be stilled. She thought back to their conversations and realized he'd never told her. He had only mentioned his name.

A tumble of confused feelings assailed her. Her emotions were out of control. If it wasn't bad enough that Sorcha reveled in being the laird's daughter and having made an alliance with the MacKays, now Ceana had to live with the fact that the man who'd kissed her and stirred her soul was marrying her dreadful cousin. This was too much. She couldn't bear anymore.

The door swung open, and Anna entered. Ceana couldn't calm her racing heart. She couldn't catch her breath. The last she remembered was falling into her sister's arms and hitting the floor with a thud.

Fingers tapped Ceana's face as she tried to open her eyes. "Ceana, wake up! Ceana!"

"I'm awake. What happened?" She held her hand to her head.

"Ye had a fainting spell. Let me help ye to the bed." Her sister pulled her to her feet, and Ceana sat on the edge of the bed.

"I'm fine."

"Ye're nae fine. Lie down before ye fall over again." Anna picked up the pendant on the floor and placed it back in the box on Ceana's dresser. Her sister sat beside her on the bed and sighed. "I can remember a conversation between us nae all that long ago. Ye were cross at me for nae telling ye about Samuel. How is it that ye know Laird MacKay's son? And before ye answer, I'd think twice about spinning tales to me."

Ceana growled. "Samuel gave his word."

"*Samuel* didnae tell me anything. Ye're my sister. I know ye, and ye knew that man."

"I met Luthais at the standing stones."

Anna's eyes lit up in surprise. "Ye went to the standing stones? I've been trying to convince Samuel to take me."

"I know. He told me all about it. I wasnae there to find a husband, if that's what ye're thinking."

"I didnae think that ye were."

Ceana rubbed the palm of her hands over her eyes. "The next day Luthais appeared at the loch and we talked."

"Please tell me ye still have your virtue."

When Ceana realized her sister was throwing her own words back at her, she gave a small smile. "I still have my virtue. One of his hawks pecked me and—"

"The man has hawks? The ones that fly over our home are his?"

"Anna, the truth of the matter is that I thought he was a MacKay guard, and he must've thought I was Uncle John's daughter."

"Why would ye tell him that?"

"I didnae tell him that."

"Oh, Ceana. This is a fine mess ye've created. What are ye going to do? Are ye in love with him?"

Ceana lifted a brow. "Love? We shared a kiss, but I barely know him. I did favor the brief time that I spent with him, but—"

"There is nay 'but.' I know he felt the same because I saw the look on his face when he found out ye werenae the woman he thought ye were. Ye more than likely donna want to hear my opinion, but it didnae take long for me to realize how much I loved Samuel. If ye care or have any feelings for Luthais, ye cannae let Sorcha have him. Ye cannae let her win again."

Anna continued. "Our uncle, aunt, and cousin have taken everything away from us. We have naught else to lose. We are Gunns. Our parents raised us well. We will nae be defeated again. Go to him. The man gazed at ye with the same look in his eye that Samuel does when he looks at me. When I saw Luthais in the bailey with his father and that verra large guard, he was distraught. I promise ye that he shares your feelings. Tell him everything and give yourself a chance at happiness…for both our sakes."

CHAPTER EIGHT

The misery of the night didn't let up and haunted Luthais to the point of madness. He felt trapped. He was suffocating on his own stupidity. His feelings were too raw to discuss with his father or Doughall. He'd formed an alliance with the Gunns based on being besotted with a woman who'd played him for a fool. His clan's future was now in his hands. If he reneged on his marriage to the true laird's daughter, not only would the Gunns and MacKays be warring clans again, but the tension would mount between them like wildfire.

Luthais sat with his back against his favorite standing stone and rubbed his hands over his face. He could not stop himself from pondering the simplest question. *Why?* Why would the lass tell him she was the laird's daughter? What could she have gained? He even remembered questioning her about the number of suitors lining up at the gates. He couldn't get over the fact that she'd blatantly lied to him.

The sky was cloudy and dark with no stars in sight.

As the torchlight illuminated the stones with an eerie glow, he felt something watching him, waiting in the shadows. He took another swig of whisky and then raised his arms in the air.

"*Trobhadaidh.*" *Come.* Two of his birds landed on his leather-strapped shoulders and Mac na Diobhail on the leather sleeve of his arm.

For a moment, Luthais paused. He thought he'd indeed gone mad. Mac na Diobhail looked like the Devil incarnate. A long tongue hung out of his bird's beak. Luthais swallowed hard, wondering if he'd opened some type of supernatural connection with his foul mood. He lifted his arm toward the light and breathed a sigh of relief when his hawk spit out what was left of a mouse.

"Mister MacKay…"

He gazed in the center of the standing stones, and there was Mistress Gunn—Ceana—looking ethereal in the dim light. The lace at her slender throat parted, and the hollow of her neck was filled with soft shadows.

"Ah, Mistress Gunn… To what do I owe the pleasure?" he asked with bitterness. His eyes clawed her like talons.

"May I speak with ye? Please." Her tone was soft.

As if on cue, Mac na Diobhail let out a scolding call. "*Dèan às!*" *Be gone!* His birds flew onto the tree branch above, but not before Mac na Diobhail picked up what was left of his meal from the ground. "I donna think it wise for ye to be here." When she stepped around the torch, he shot her a withering glance. "I wouldnae get too close."

"I'll take my chances."

Luthais actually meant "close to the fire" but had no desire to correct what she thought. Perhaps that's what had gotten him into all this trouble in the first place. She sat beside him, and the scent of lavender invaded his senses.

"I need to explain, and I wish for ye to hear me out."

He shook his head at her audacity in coming here to try to give a reason for why she'd lied in the first place. He took another sip of whisky and wiped his mouth with the back of his hand. He couldn't help it when he chuckled nastily. "What good would that do me now, eh? Believe me, I donna need to hear any more of your words. I've heard enough."

"Mister MacK...er, Luthais, in my defense, I ne'er knew ye were Laird MacKay's son. I thought ye were a guard, the same as the giant man with the red hair."

"I want to know why ye told me ye were the laird's daughter." He spoke between clenched teeth and she gazed down, fingering her cloak with a nervous gesture.

"I ne'er said that I was. What I told ye at the loch was that ye'd better take your leave before my father's men came and found ye." When he looked at her like he didn't believe a word she said, the lass continued. "My father *was* laird. He was killed two years ago, along with my mother. Men attacked their coach on the road, robbing my parents and leaving them for dead."

Although it took an inordinate amount of strength not reach out and throttle Ceana, he felt a moment of sympathy for her. They shared a common bond. "Please accept my apologies for the loss of your parents. My mother passed as well and some days 'tis difficult without her, but that still doesnae make this situation even close to being better."

She reached out to touch him and then, as if she had second thoughts, withdrew her hand. "After my parents passed, Uncle John, Father's brother, became laird. He wasted nay time removing all of my parents' belongings, even taking down my father's portrait from the wall." Tears fell down her cheeks, and Luthais resisted the urge to wipe them.

"The manner in which my uncle banished all the memories of my parents was as if they'd ne'er existed. My sire was such a caring laird, a doting husband, and a loving father. I cannae say the same for my uncle. For the past two years, he's ne'er wanted—nor has he felt the need—to worry or concern himself about Anna, my sister, or me. 'Twas if we were being punished because our parents died and left us behind."

As if Ceana realized she'd wandered far from the path of the conversation long ago, she shook her head. "When ye found me here at the stones, I thought ye were a guard chasing me off MacKay lands. Then when ye told me your name was Luthais MacKay, I thought the same."

This time she reached out, and the touch of her hand was almost unbearable in its tenderness. He grasped her fingers and couldn't find the strength to pull away, even though he knew he should. He rubbed his thumb gently back and forth.

"The truth is, Luthais MacKay, I didnae care then and I donna care now if ye are the laird's son or a MacKay guard. I favor ye, and I ne'er meant for any of this to happen. I seem to have a way about me where everything in my life goes awry."

He almost laughed at the irony.

"My uncle has taken everything away that I hold dear. I want ye to know that I've ne'er kissed—nor have I ever been with—another man. I need ye to understand that I—"

"God's teeth, Ceana! Do ye think I want to wed your cousin? I wanted to wed *ye*! I have been placed in a horrible predicament. I will be laird of the MacKays one day. I have to think of the best interests of my clan and nae look at what I want or what I desire to have. An alliance between the Gunns and the MacKays would—"

She placed her fingers to his lips. "Luthais," she said, giving him a gentle smile. "My father was a great man. He always looked after our clan. I am aware of the responsibilities of a Highland laird. I also recognize that this entire situation is of my own doing." She paused. "I donna like it at all, but I know ye have to wed my cousin." She wept aloud. "But it breaks my heart at the thought of losing ye."

In one forward motion, Luthais pulled Ceana into his arms and pressed his lips to hers. His tongue traced the soft fullness of her lips and then explored her mouth. He shifted and kissed the pulsing hollow at the base of her throat as blood coursed through her veins.

Ceana became instantly awake.

His arms encircled her, one hand at the small of her back. She could feel his uneven breathing on her cheek as he held her close. The warmth of his arms was so male, so bracing. His mouth was warm and sweet on hers. The mere touch of his hand sent a warming shiver through her, and she tingled from the contact. She felt transported on a soft and wispy cloud.

His demanding lips caressed her, and his slow, drugging kisses were driving her mad. With his tongue, he ravished her mouth. He released her briefly, only enough to breathe, and then repeated his ritual. Raising his mouth from hers, he gazed into her eyes.

"If we donna stop now, I cannae be responsible for my actions. I will take your virtue and ruin ye for any other man."

She placed her forehead to his, panting. "I was ruined for any other man the day that I met ye, Luthais MacKay."

He slid her day dress off her shoulders and down her arms, so that she lay bare beneath his sultry glance. Then he tugged off his tunic and hastily tossed it aside.

Ceana gasped as bare skin met bare skin and she felt her breasts crush against the hardness of his chest.

Luthais picked up a lock of her hair and caressed it gently. "Ye are so verra bonny."

When he lightly kneaded her breasts with his rough fingers and teased her nipples into hard, aching points, her mind was robbed of any coherent words. He lowered his head and kissed her taut buds, rousing a melted sweetness within her. She found it difficult to remain still when he suckled the tips of her breasts.

There was a heated swelling between her legs, a moistness she did not understand.

When he slid his hand over her trembling stomach and then between her legs, she froze. He kissed her again and, with a few skillful strokes of his fingers, alleviated her shock at how personally he was touching her. His finger thrust inside her, imitating the movement of his tongue in her mouth.

He felt so strong against her body that she was completely enthralled by his masculinity. The possessiveness of his touch did not lessen her awareness of the man in her arms. In truth, she sensed a sudden secureness, protectiveness, coming from him. Is this what it would've meant to be husband and wife? Her mind was so cluttered with thoughts that she wasn't exactly sure what she was experiencing.

Luthais's body moved to partially cover hers, his hands lifting her skirts above her hips. He reached down and loosened his kilt while he continued to drug her with passionate kisses. She was more than a little nervous, but he continued to distract her in pleasant ways.

He eased himself inside her and, with one quick thrust, made her his.

Ceana gasped as he held himself up on his forearms, fighting to remain still. His body shook with strain, and sweat beaded on his forehead. When she moved beneath him, he pressed his head to hers.

"God, lass. I'm trying nae to hurt ye. Please donna move. Ye're going to unman me."

She wasn't sure what she was doing wrong, but he grasped her by the calves and gently pushed her legs up until her knees were bent. When he pressed deeper within her, she clamped her eyes shut and not from the pain.

He reached down and rubbed her most sensitive spot. Their bodies were in exquisite harmony with one another. A hunger inched through her veins, rousing her to the peak of desire. She wanted to yield to the burning sweetness that was captive within her.

The passion of his ardor mounted, and she finally abandoned herself to the whirl of sensations. Love flowed into her like warm, molten honey, shattering her into a million glowing stars.

Sorcha Gunn knocked on her cousin's bedchamber door. She hesitated and then rapped again. Then, raising the latch, she took a peek inside. When she saw the room was dark, she said a silent prayer of thanks. She entered, closing the door behind her, and hastily made her way to the other side of the bed. If she was caught, there would be no escaping punishment for her actions this time. Lifting the feather mattress, she pulled out her cousin's journal and walked to the desk. She would never have found the book if she hadn't been searching for the dress she thought her cousin had stolen.

She fumbled for the candle and, once it was lit, flipped through the pages of the journal toward the end. Ceana thought she was clever, but Sorcha knew her cousin was nothing but simpleminded. Ceana and Sorcha's new betrothed may have fooled everyone in the great hall, but Sorcha knew the two of them had known each other. A blind idiot could see that. She only needed proof, and then she'd demand that her cousins be sent away. She didn't give a damn where. Quickly scanning the pages of her cousin's journal, Sorcha's eyes froze on a passage.

There it was.

Her daft cousin had written her thoughts in print. Not only was Ceana acquainted with Luthais MacKay, but they'd even shared a kiss. This was all the evidence Sorcha needed to get rid of her nemesis once and for all. She blew out the candle and carried the journal as if it were a sacred text. Making her way through the halls of the castle, she smiled as she passed her father's portrait. She would always be her father's daughter.

Sorcha was about to knock on her father's study door when raised voices came from within. Needing a private moment with her father, she didn't want to interrupt him and then have to explain why she was there in front of someone else. She placed her ear to the door, hoping the person inside was her mother.

"Ye still think the alliance with the MacKays will secure our future?"

"First, we must get them to trust us. That MacKay dog will nae even know his daughter-by-marriage betrayed him," said her father. "I've been trying to seize MacKay lands for years, and now they'll be mine for the taking. 'Tis about damn time."

"And if your daughter fails? Ye could always kill the MacKay and his son like ye did your brother and his wife. Shouldnae be too difficult to make it look like an accident or as if another clan was responsible."

"Donna worry about Sorcha. She will nae fail. She'll do anything that her father tells her to do."

Sorcha gazed down at the journal that was now stained with her tears. She was breathless with rage and hurt. She swung open the door, not giving a damn who was behind it. She glared at her father and Raonull with burning, reproachful eyes. Fury almost choked her.

"Daughter, whatever are ye doing, and what do ye

have there?"

She shut the door behind her with a heavy blow. "Sit down, Father." The long look the two of them exchanged incensed her even more. Her expression became thunderous. "Ye too, Raonull. We all need to have a wee chat."

CHAPTER NINE

Luthais reined in his mount beside Ceana as the sun started to rise above the horizon. He'd never seen her look as beautiful as with her tousled hair and swollen lips. Satisfaction pursed his mouth, knowing he was responsible for her appearance. He winked when he caught her eye.

"Ye didnae sleep in your bed last eve. Will your sister be worried? Mayhap your uncle will send men out to find ye."

"I doubt anyone, including my uncle, will even notice that I'm gone."

He gathered his thoughts before he spoke again. "Are ye all right? Did I hurt ye?"

"The only part of me that aches is my heart. I'll truly miss ye, Luthais. I wish there was a way we could be together." She straightened herself in the saddle. "But my cousin will soon be your wife, and ye have a duty to your clan."

He offered her a comforting smile. "There still may be a chance for us."

"And what is that, pray tell?"

"We kissed, and we both touched *na tursachan* at the same time. Mayhap fate will save us both and we'll be husband and wife, be as one."

Ceana waved him off. "If ye're going to tell me that my fallen tears will turn the heather beneath my feet white, then I'm glad we didnae wed."

"Pardon?"

She shrugged. "Malvina."

"I donna understand."

"Nor do I when people believe in legends and tales of kissing at a stone when they should know better. Fate is what ye make it."

Luthais couldn't say that he disagreed. When they reached the border, he stopped and dismounted. He assisted Ceana from her horse and didn't miss the touch of sadness that crossed her face. His fingers brushed her cheek.

"I donna think it wise for me to travel any farther. This isnae right, lass. I took your innocence. Ye should be my wife. If ye are with child—" He heard his voice and it sounded unnatural.

"And your clan would be warring with mine if ye refused to wed Sorcha." She grabbed his hand and closed her eyes. "I want to take a moment longer. I want to remember our time together, ye, and the way we are now." Her gaze met his. "Luthais, I—"

Ceana flung herself away from him at the sound of thundering hoofbeats and at the sight of his betrothed.

Ceana watched in horror as Sorcha dismounted and approached them with a wicked smile. *Good God!* What could Ceana possibly say now since she'd been caught in the arms of her cousin's betrothed? She shifted from foot to foot and stole a quick glance at Luthais as he stepped forward.

"Mistress Gunn, what a pleasant surprise to see ye—"

She held up her hand. "Please save your words for someone who believes them." Sorcha's accusing gaze was riveted on Ceana, but then she turned and narrowed her eyes at Luthais. "Do ye love my cousin?"

His eyebrows shot up in surprise. "Pardon?"

"I donna have time for games. I asked ye a question, and I deserve an honest response." She placed her hands on her hips, waiting for an answer.

"I only met your cousin yester—"

"I know ye kissed her at the loch, and I also know that Ceana's ne'er felt this way before about anyone. Ye made her heart 'sing with delight,'" said Sorcha in a singing tone. "Those were your words. Were they nae?" She turned, smiling at Ceana.

"How could ye possibly know that?" Ceana didn't realize that her voice went up a notch or two. Sorcha walked to her mount and ruffled through a satchel. As she came back, she lifted a brow and held out Ceana's journal. "*Bàs an fhithich ort!*" *May you suffer the death of the raven!*

"To be truthful, I'm surprised ye didnae curse me with hawks, Cousin. But aye, I spent the night reading your journal. In the future, ye may nae want to write down all your thoughts so anyone can find them, or at least find a better place to hide your book." She handed Ceana back her journal. "But that's nae the reason I'm here." Sorcha turned to Luthais and placed her hand on his arm.

He stiffened at the gesture.

"I know ye're going to be verra disappointed with what I've come to say, but I'm afraid that I simply cannae marry ye. Ye must know that I've had many suitors from which to choose. I'm ashamed to admit that I havenae really given this subject the amount of thought that I should. In short, I've agreed too hastily to be wed. I dare say we are now in quite the quandary."

Sorcha turned to Ceana and sighed. "The Gunns have made an alliance with the MacKays, and now that the betrothal is broken, I'm afraid so is the agreement. Unless of course, Mister MacKay weds another Gunn." She shrugged. "Then I suppose the alliance would be restored and all would be well."

A warning voice whispered in Ceana's head. "What is this about, Sorcha? I donna understand what ye're doing. Does Uncle John know about this? He would ne'er let ye—"

"What about my father? He's aware that I refuse to wed Mister MacKay." Sorcha smiled at Luthais.

"Please take nay offense."

Luthais' eyes shifted from Sorcha to Ceana.

"Father has even given ye his blessing to marry Mister MacKay. If Mister MacKay wants to wed ye, of course."

"I want naught more in this world." Luthais smiled at Sorcha. "Please take nay offense."

Ceana's mind raced with new ideas, but she was in too much shock to even put two words together to form a coherent sentence. This was all occurring so fast. What could've possibly happened from last eve until now to have Fate change its fickle mind—and her cousin's?

The standing stones.

Sorcha brushed her hands together. "Good. Now that that's settled, Mister MacKay, might I have a private word with ye?"

Luthais had no idea what Sorcha was about. A voice in the back of his mind whispered not to trust her. Now that Ceana had left them, he intended to find out the truth. He whirled on Sorcha.

"I swear if ye—"

"Please save your threats, Mister MacKay. I released ye from your troth, but in return ye must do something for me." Something cautioned him not to ask, and when Sorcha lifted the edge of her skirts, he averted his eyes. "I want ye to take this." When he looked back, she handed him a letter that was sealed with wax. "Ye will hide that document as if your life depended on it. And please realize that keeping it under the mattress of your bed isnae a good place."

He wasn't about to admit that was the first thought that came to mind.

"Give me your word that ye will nae read or open that letter. If ye do, ye place in danger the lives of those who ye love the most."

"Aye, I give ye my word, but what are the contents?"

"If something befalls me, then and only then may ye read the letter and show it to Ceana."

He lifted a brow, and a puzzled expression crossed his face. "What could possibly befall ye? Are *ye* in danger?"

"I'm afraid that I've treated my cousins terribly." She started to walk back toward her mount and turned her head over her shoulder. "I am making things right, Mister MacKay."

A fortnight later Ceana stood at the altar with Luthais, pinching herself twice to make sure this was real. He looked so handsome in his MacKay plaid. His long hair was tied back at the nape of his neck. She could've done without the leather that was strapped to his arm, but at least he'd removed the ones at his shoulders before their wedding.

She smiled at her sister and Samuel as they sat in a pew side by side. She shook her head at Aunt Marta chanting some new incantation under her breath. And she even smiled at Sorcha who was sitting next to brooding Uncle John. Ceana wasn't sure how her cousin had managed to convince the man to become so agreeable, but she was glad she had. Perhaps there was hope of saving Sorcha's soul yet.

When the priest asked for the rings, the doors to the chapel swung open with a loud bang, and Luthais' large, redheaded friend gave a nod in the breadth of the doors. Ceana almost laughed because the man barely fit between them.

Luthais shouted, *"Trobhad!" Come!*

Mac na Bracha flew in through the open chapel doors and landed on Luthais's arm. The bird carried a small bag around its neck.

Luthais lifted his arm to Ceana and smiled. "Ye'll need to remove the rings, lass." As soon as Ceana untied the tiny bag, he said, *"Dèan às!" Be gone!* The hawk flew out the doors, and Ceana heard a large gasp. She wasn't sure if the sound came from the Gunns or the MacKays who were in attendance.

She thought she had spoken her vows. She vaguely remembered exchanging the rings. The only thing Ceana knew for certain was that she and Luthais were now husband and wife. His hands slipped up her arms, bringing her closer.

"Come here, Wife."

As though his words released her, Ceana flung herself against him. "I love ye, Luthais."

"And I love ye."

He lowered his head, and their love was sealed with a kiss or by a standing stone. For the first time in her life, Ceana wasn't sure which.

ALSO AVAILABLE
BY
VICTORIA ROBERTS

Bad Boys of the Highlands series
Temptation in a Kilt—Book One
X Marks the Scot—Book Two
To Wed a Wicked Highlander—Book Three

Highland Spies series
My Highland Spy—Book One
Kilts and Daggers—Book Two
Kill or Be Kilt—Book Three

Kilts and Kisses novella series
Kilts and Kisses—Novella One
(Previously published in the
Kissing the Highlander anthology)

ABOUT THE AUTHOR

Award-winning author Victoria Roberts writes Scottish historical romances about kilted heroes and warriors from the past. She was the recipient of the 2013 *RT Book Reviews* Reviewers' Choice award for Best Medieval Historical Romance for *X Marks the Scot*, as well as the 2014 *BTS Book Reviews* Red Carpet award for Best Historical and Best Book of the Year for *My Highland Spy*. Victoria is a member of Romance Writers of America and several local chapters, in addition to being a contributing author to the online magazine *Celtic Guide*. When she's not plotting her next Scottish adventure, she's dragging her clan to every Scottish festival under the sun. Visit Victoria at **VictoriaRobertsAuthor.com**.

CPSIA information can be obtained
at www.ICGtesting.com
Printed in the USA
LVHW091338030119
602624LV00001B/12/P

9 781517 044329